Open Up

by the same author

We Don't Know What We're Doing

Thomas Morris
OPEN UP

faber

First published in 2023
by Faber & Faber Limited
The Bindery, 51 Hatton Garden
London EC1N 8HN

Typeset by Faber & Faber Limited
Printed and bound in the UK by CPI Group (UK) Ltd, Croydon, CR0 4YY

*Open Up is a work of fiction. All characters, organisations and events
portrayed in these stories are either products of the author's imagination or
are used fictitiously. Any resemblance to real life is entirely inevitable.*

A CIP record for this book
is available from the British Library

ISBN 978–0–571–31704–2

2 4 6 8 10 9 7 5 3 1

Contents

The facts are sonorous but between the facts there's a whispering. It's the whispering that astounds me.

- Clarice Lispector, *Hour of the Star*
(trans. Benjamin Moser)

OPEN UP

Wales

It's been three months since they saw each other, and Gareth wonders if his father will recognise him. He pictures his mother upstairs, sitting at her dressing table, practising her face. He wonders if his father will come into the house. He thinks: if Dad comes in, Wales will lose.

Hearing his mother on the stairs, he moves from the window and settles on the couch – the gap in the curtains the only evidence he was standing there, waiting for his father's car.

Got your phone? she asks.

Yep.

Text when you're on your way back, alright?

Yeah yeah, he says.

A car horn beeps outside: his father has arrived – and he isn't coming in.

There's a pause, then his mother smiles.

Well, have a good time, she says. And make sure you get something to eat. I've told your father, but you know what he's like.

Gareth nods, absorbs it all. If Wales win tonight, everything will turn out okay. His mother will find a wad of cash stuffed in the walls and they won't need to move out. But if Wales lose, the repo man – with his bulging muscles

3

– will return and take Gareth's bike. Or the ceiling will cave in and fall down on him while he's watching cartoons on the couch.

Wouldn't it be mad if you see me in the crowd on the telly? he says.

His mother grins.

I'll keep an eye out for you, she says.

Outside, the March evening air is fresh on his cheeks.

Young man, his father says in greeting.

Alright? Gareth replies.

They drive up Caerphilly Mountain, Gareth secretly studying his father's head. One day he'll be able to read people's minds. He just needs to learn to focus harder.

What you looking at? his father asks.

I think you're going bald, Gareth says.

Wonderful, his father replies. Another thing for me to worry about.

They drive on. When they hit traffic, his father instructs Gareth to open the glove compartment, where he finds the two tickets, sacred and shiny: his first real match at a real stadium.

So what do we know about Northern Ireland? his father asks. Any predictions?

They've got some good defenders, Gareth says. But Wales will win. I'm gonna say . . . two–nil. Ramsey header and . . . a Gareth Bale bikey from the halfway.

His father laughs, then in a quiet voice explains that

because it's only a friendly, Ramsey and Bale have been rested and won't be playing.

Oh right, Gareth says.

It'll still be a good game. Just don't get your hopes up, alright? And put those tickets back now, before you lose them.

His father refuses to pay for parking, so for twenty minutes they drive round one residential avenue after another, finally finding a spot in a street lined with trees.

Let's just hope we can remember where we're parked, his father says, as they walk past houses three storeys tall, with tiled porches and coloured glass in the doors.

They're lovely houses, Gareth says.

They'd probably cost you . . . pfft . . . a million pounds? his father says.

A million quid! Gareth says. That's insane, that is.

They walk on, Gareth taking two steps for every one of his dad's.

Slow down, will you? I'm literally only ten.

Well, hold my hand then.

Nah, you're alright, Gareth says.

On the high street, the air throbs with horns and whistles. Crowds with flags draped over their shoulders spill into the road, the cars slowing and honking. Outside a pub, a group of men in red T-shirts toot trumpets and trombones, and one man plays the sax and another bangs a drum. Arms aloft, the fans sing *I LOVE YOU BABY!* and a woman, dressed like a daffodil, jumps up and down, her pint spilling onto the pavement.

Let's get some grub, his father says.

They eat outside the chippy, leaning against the window. The chips are hot and moist with vinegar. Inside, a girl with a red dragon stencilled on her cheek stands beside her dad, with a burger and a can of Coke. If she looks at Gareth, Wales will win.

Enjoying the chips? his father asks.

Yeah, Gareth says. They're lovely.

As they're about to leave, the girl smiles through the glass.

Onwards they go now, among the stream of fans, down sneaky avenues and busy roads, onwards towards the stadium. Wearing coats and scarves and bucket hats the fans sing, *Don't take me home, please don't take me home, I just don't want to go to work.* Up above, the sky is purple black.

It's a long walk, Gareth says.

Best way to soak up the atmosphere, his father replies.

You should have parked closer to the stadium, Gareth says. This is a bloody marathon.

Football is all about opinions, his father says. And in my opinion: you can shut up.

Gareth laughs, and the crowd shoals through the dark streets until suddenly the stadium is before them, glowing like a flying saucer. His father buys a programme and Gareth holds it proudly. In the queue, a bald security guard shouts, COATS OFF! ARMS IN THE AIR! He looks like the repo man, the man who took away his mother's car.

Alright son? he asks, patting Gareth down. Any knives in your pockets?

As if! Gareth replies.

Good boy, the man says, smiling. Have a good game.

Through the beeping turnstiles now, into what feels like an underground car park. Bodies hassle past, and there's the smell of sizzling onions and hotdogs. A woman in a high-vis jacket checks their tickets and directs them up a flight of concrete steps, and then they are somehow, magically, outside again, and there it is – the pitch! It's way different to how it looks on the telly. The grass is a giant green stage; lit so bright beneath the floodlights, it seems unreal.

Their seats are behind the goals. As the players warm up, he feels the thud of each kick in his chest, and he hears the coaches' echoing shouts. He pictures stepping onto the grass, striking a penalty, the net rippling.

When the anthem begins, they rise to their feet, and his father's voice is deep and rumbling. Gareth has sung it in school before, but this is completely different. The anthem is massive, it fills his chest and roars out of him as if everything – Wales, the world, his whole life – depends on it. At the end, his father claps and yells C'MON WALES. And Gareth yells it too, then bellows the chant that's whirling around the stadium: WALES! WALES! He is screaming, he is letting something go.

The game is difficult to follow. There are no video replays, no commentators, just the players on the pitch and the sound of the crowd. For every Wales tackle, a swelling roar fills the air, and any decision against them means thousands of people howling at the referee. The crowd urge the players and the players drive the crowd, and it's electric, and it feels out of control. The match is a blur and before he knows it, it's half-time.

Nil–nil, his father says.

They leave their seats and head back out to the concourse. Gareth blows on his hands to warm them up. His father asks if he wants a hot chocolate, but Gareth says he needs a wee.

At the urinals, sandwiched between two men, nothing comes out. Beside him, a man sways and leans on the wall to steady himself. Gareth does up his zip and comes back to his dad.

Did you go?

Yeah, Gareth lies.

Wash your hands then.

At the sink, he sends his special energy to the players. When he was four years old, he got separated from his Mum in WHSmiths. Looking for the DVDs, he found a narrow blue corridor. He passed through alone. The floor was slanted and everything was so, so quiet and he realised he had entered a secret realm between this world and another. Years passed before he emerged beside his mum at the stationery. Later, at home, he tested his powers: with his hands above his head, he stood still in the corner of the living room. His father walked past and did not see him, and Gareth only returned to the world when his mother called him for his dinner.

*

As the team run out for the second half, Gareth closes his eyes and transmits messages: come on, he tells them. We can do this. And it seems to work – Wales play well, but then Northern Ireland start to attack, and the fans begin muttering. And in the 60th minute, when Northern Ireland score, all the air is sucked out of the stadium.

I bloody knew it, his father says.

The crowd falls silent, except for the few hundred cheering green shirts in the corner.

His heart is a bashed-up football. Every time Wales get possession, it's just a matter of time until Northern Ireland take it back. With every Northern Ireland attack, he pictures them scoring.

This won't do. It just won't do. He tells himself to shape up, to focus, to really try his best. With his mind, he keeps pulling the ball towards the Northern Ireland end. He focuses and focuses, and he wishes and he wishes, and he summons all the magic in his body. But it's no use: on the clock, 70 minutes become 75 becomes 80. There's only ten minutes left. If Wales lose, he just knows that something terrible will happen. He breathes deep, and this is it: he focuses on the ball, he wills it, insists with all his power, and with one minute to go Simon Church is in the box, and Gareth screams GO ON! and Church touches the ball away from the defender, then tumbles – and with a sharp whistle, the referee awards Wales a penalty.

Oh my god, Gareth says.

His father turns his back.

I can't look, he says.

9

Please, Gareth says to himself. Please, please, please.

Hands on hips, Simon Church tries to compose himself, and Gareth is back in the blue corridor, the timeless place between worlds, where it's quiet and still, and everything is at his command.

When Church runs up and sweeps the ball into the net, the stadium erupts and Gareth roars YES, and his father hugs him tight, his stubble bristling Gareth's cheek.

Then the referee blows for full time, and the game ends one-all.

They stay behind to clap the players and the manager off the pitch. Gareth waves, but Chris Coleman doesn't see him.

Exiting the stadium, the night air feels raw on his face, and his legs are aching.

And now for the marathon back to the car, Gareth says.

Don't you start now, his father says. God, we were terrible tonight. If we play like that in the Euros we've got no hope.

Neither Gareth nor his father know this, but in four months' time, on a July afternoon, they'll come back to the stadium and cheer the Wales team on their return from the European Championships. For Gareth, it will have been a summer of dizzy days and holy nights watching Wales play football on the telly. He'll watch one game with his dad, one game with his mum, and he'll even watch a game with his friends in the hall at school. And when the repo man comes – and takes the TV, and the bank repossesses the house, and Gareth and his mum move in with Aunty Avril – they'll watch the Quarter Final in Avril's living room. Gareth will wear his lucky socks, reeling around the carpet every time Wales score. And when Wales are finally knocked out in the Semi-Finals, he'll collapse on the bed he shares with his mother and cry. Afterwards, when she comes in and strokes his head, he'll say to her: I'm not sad. I just feel proud.

But right now, they don't know any of this. The summer is way off. It is March, the start of spring, the air still chilled with winter. But the evenings are stretching, and the days are warming, and Gareth, you can feel the change already, can't you? That feeling is coming back, the belief that your life is forever on the cusp of magic. Walking with the crowd now, watching your father's breath curl white into the dark night as the flowing fans chant and sing for Wales, you know, somehow, that everything will be okay. It's a private feeling, fizzing like a sparkler inside your chest. Thinking about it makes you laugh.

What's so funny? your father says. Share the joke.

It's nothing, you say.

No, go on, your dad says, tell me.

Well, I've just got this feeling we're gonna do amazing at the Euros.

Your father blows out his cheeks.

Look, he says. I don't want to be a downer, but I've supported Wales a *long* time now. Honestly, it's better not to expect anything. They'll only let you down in the end.

Actually, that's probably not a bad life lesson: you're better off not expecting much, or you'll only be disappointed.

At that, you stop and look him in the eye.

Yeah well, you say. Football is all about opinions and in my opinion you should just shut up.

Your father smiles, then laughs, and hand in hand, together you make your way back through the city, back the way you came, back in search of the car.

Aberkariad

Rhiannon once asked me if I was angry at my parents for everything that happened. I told her I wasn't. But the real answer is, I don't know. The rare times I've allowed myself to feel anger it has felt like a betrayal. So I try not to go there. I avoid the deep waters and mostly keep to the shallows. But recently, late at night especially, I've found myself drifting downwards, down to the depths where the waters are dark, and I go round in circles, the sorry hurt washing through me until my body is heavy and solemn. When I'm down there, I feel incapable of love, not worthy of it, not up to the task. I think: if love is an inheritance, then I've been given something faulty.

It was on a shrimp hunt that I first heard of Aberkariad.

Uncle Nol had taken us out for the day, and after the first twenty or so feeds, he instructed us to take a break. Hitched on thick yellow fronds in a forest of kelp, he regaled my brothers and me with stories of his travels. When he mentioned Aberkariad we must have looked dumbfounded.

'I should have known,' he said. 'Your father hasn't told you about it, has he?'

'No,' I said. 'What are Aberkariad?'

'Oh, boys bach!' Uncle Nol said, and his eyes turned outwards in disbelief. 'Let me tell you! Aberkariad is the region where the two territories overlap and *our* waters commingle with *theirs*. It's the dizziest dream made real. It's where you fill your pouch and dance until your head is spinning and your fins are in a twist.'

'Aber-*kariad*,' my brother Aled repeated, and the way he said 'Aberkariad', it sounded almost enchanted. He heard in it a music that the rest of us couldn't.

'I still don't get it,' Hywel said.

Uncle Nol clicked his mouth. 'Bloody hell boys, what is that father of yours teaching you?'

'He teaches us loads,' I said.

'Yeah?' Nol said. 'Like what?'

'Hunting plankton,' Berwyn replied coolly. 'The secret is keeping still.'

'And he's taught us all about the importance of rest and sleep,' Llwyd added, quite pleased with himself.

Uncle Nol sighed. 'Hunting and sleeping are vital, obviously. But what I'm on about is a lot more important. And a lot more exciting, too. It's about life, boys.'

'Lies!' Ieuan said.

'I don't lie,' Uncle Nol replied, and then sensing Aled rustling at his side, he turned to him. 'Young buck, what am I talking about?'

'Females?' Aled ventured.

'Got it in one, son!' Uncle Nol cried. 'Aberkariad is the place we go to meet and mate with the fillies. And

14

I'm telling you now boys, it's the greatest place in the sea.'

'Yes!' Aled shouted, and he twirled 360 in celebration.

Uncle Nol's mouth widened into a smile. 'Seriously, boys, if I could die anywhere, well – bloody hell, what a place to expire. Hot horses all over the shop.'

Buoyed by Uncle Nol and Aled's excitement, my brothers started giggling and bashing their heads together.

'Ask your father about it tonight,' Uncle Nol said. 'It's about time he started letting go.'

'Letting go of what?' I said.

Uncle Nol looked at me, and craned his thick neck, as if considering something. 'I think that's a conversation for another day,' he said. And then, turning to the boys, he called out: 'Let's get back to the hunting, is it? Those shrimpy pricks ain't gonna eat themselves.'

Leaving the forest, I asked Aled why he was so taken with the idea of Aberkariad and fillies – because I couldn't see the appeal.

'It's about doing what we are born to do,' he said. And then, inflating himself with gas, the better to show off his newly emerged brood pouch, he added: 'It's about finally filling up this hole.'

That evening, at home in the living room, Aled asked Father about visiting Aberkariad.

'Can we go tomorrow?'

'There's not a worm's chance,' Father growled. 'Aberkariad is no place for young foals.'

'But we're five months old!'

'You're still too young for what goes on there,' Father said.

Hywel got involved then. 'But me and Aled already have brood pouches. We're studs!'

'Oh for crying out loud,' Father said. 'A brood pouch doesn't make you a stud.'

'Then what does?' Aled asked.

'What have I always told you?' Father replied. 'Millions of young fry die every year simply because their fathers abandon them. Ignore what Uncle Nol tells you, and take my word for it: there's more to being an adult than screwing.'

But if my brothers were listening, Father's words didn't seem to register. A few minutes later Aled yelled, 'Starfish!' and they all quickly joined their tails together at different angles, and glided off through the ocean, slowly floating away from me and my father, singing as Aled led them in song: '*Aberkariad* – wooh! *Aberkariad* – wooh!'

Before I heard about Aberkariad, I had never questioned how exactly love would find me. Father always made it sound inevitable: when the time was right, we would meet the right partner – someone special with whom we'd form a life bond – and then we would love and be loved for the rest of our days.

It was presented as something ordained and natural, like the way the light of the rising sun coursed orange through the waters at dawn; and how the waters brightened as the sun climbed higher and the day turned yellow; and how the waters eventually faded golden with sunset, until finally everything darkened, and we basked on coral in the diffracted light of the bare lonesome moon.

'Let them go, mun,' Uncle Nol was saying a few weeks later. 'Let them go to Aberkariad.'

We were in the living room again, gathered around Father as he worked on a portrait of Mother. In this one, she appeared side-on: her curvy white tail wrapped around a long blade of grass, a serene smile lighting her face. Many such portraits lined the whalebone shelves of our home, and in each picture Mother looked so warm and so friendly I felt as if I knew her.

'Please, Dad,' Ieuan said, inflating his own new brood pouch. 'Let us go to Aberkariad!'

'It's not the right time for you boys,' Father replied. 'You're just not ready yet.'

'Of course they're bloody ready,' Uncle Nol said. 'They're six months old.'

'I'm talking emotionally,' Father said.

'Oh here we go,' Uncle Nol said. 'Captain Loveheart strikes again.'

'Mock me all you like,' Father said.

'Thank you,' Uncle Nol said. 'I will.'

Father ignored the comment. He simply gazed down at the portrait and applied delicate strokes to the dorsal stripe on Mother's back. I too had the same stripe on my back, and was secretly thrilled that I was the only one of my brothers to have inherited it.

'Seriously, though,' Uncle Nol said, 'your behaviour is just so unmale. How did you ever grow so attached to one partner?'

'It's called love,' Father said. 'It's called honouring a commitment. She'll be back soon, once the seasons change. The waters are just a bit choppy right now.'

Uncle Nol shook his head and tutted.

'You really need to get back out there, mun,' he said. 'You've got to meet someone new.'

Father laughed. 'As much as I appreciate this little pep-talk, I'm quite content, thank you very much.'

Uncle Nol shook his head and turned to us.

'You know what, boys? Your father should be doing *my* portrait. Because without horses like me, there'd be no bloody species left.'

Father gave no reply.

He simply smiled to himself, dipped the stem of his reed into his dish of octopus ink, and continued with his painting.

That night, at supper, Aled again pushed Father on the topic of Aberkariad. He wanted to know if Aberkariad was where he had met our mother.

'It was indeed,' Father answered.

'Then why deny us that same chance for love?'

'I'm not denying you that,' Father replied. 'I just think you should wait a little bit longer. There's still some things you need to learn.'

'Like what?' Ieuan said.

'Well, for starters: the importance of taking responsibility,' Father said. 'My own father abandoned me soon as I was born. Can you imagine what that was like? Can you imagine how different life would be for you boys if I hadn't been around to look after you all?'

'Plenty of other horses live like that, and they're just fine,' Aled said. 'Look at Uncle Nol!'

'Listen,' Father answered, 'your Uncle Nol was affected as much by our father's leaving as I was. But he just deals with it differently. To come into the world without a clue of who you are or what you're meant to do . . . I . . . I just don't think you ever get over it.'

'But it's so common though,' Berwyn said. 'Almost every horse has to deal with it.'

'I know,' Father replied, 'but just because an experience is common, it doesn't make it any less painful to go through. And when I became a father, I made a vow to do things differently. I promised myself – and I promised your mother too – that I would stick around and support my children. And you know what? I don't regret it. Every *single* day I am happy and grateful that I made that choice.'

To which Aled replied: 'Yeah, and look where it got you.'

'What does that mean?'

'You're here on your own, aren't you? And where the hell is Mam?'

'She's coming back,' Father said.

'But how do you know?' Ieuan said. 'How can you say that?'

'Because she's not like other horses,' Father replied. 'She has a good light within her, and the good light will guide her home. Just as soon as the seasons change. The waters are just too rough right now.'

Berwyn said: 'But if most horses leave their fry, then how can it be wrong?'

Father looked at us earnestly. 'Just because something is normal, it doesn't mean it's right.'

'Now I'm confused,' I said. 'Does that mean Mother is a bad horse or what?'

'Oh boys bach,' Father said. 'Your mother didn't leave you. She just hasn't come back yet. Your mother is a wonderful horse.'

'If she's so wonderful,' Aled said, 'then how come she isn't here right now?'

Father sighed.

'Ah crabs,' he said. 'I can see I need to tell this story from the start.'

This is what our father told us:

The moment he was thrust into this life, the first thing

he saw was his father's back as he swam away and abandoned him. Immediately, Father said, he felt within himself a gaping lack that throbbed to his core.

Of all his surviving siblings, Nol was the only one he found. Alone and tiny in a vast sea, they joined tails and vowed to always stick together.

And so they swam on, hunting together, feeding together, and resting together when they were tired. It wasn't an easy life, but it was good to have someone by his side.

However, as the tides turned, they met new horses and they made new friends, and Uncle Nol began to meet and mate with fillies. Each time, the same thing would happen – Nol would get pregnant, give birth, abandon the fry, and each time he and Father would have the same argument: how could Nol do this when he knew exactly how it felt to come into the world alone?

Uncle Nol's response was to laugh and tell Father to lighten up ('Your skin's getting so grey!') and he kept urging him to just mate with someone, anyone. So for a while Father went on dates and he met with fillies, and . . . well . . . they were all great horses in their own right, but in their company he never experienced the surging force he knew he was meant to feel.

He sang to us then from his favourite folk song:

> Come to me, the wave of love
> Wash over me, from high above
> Carry me to distant waters

And carry me to secret shores
For I long to meet the one who'll tell me
'You are mine – and I am yours'

He said he wanted more from life than a succession of casual encounters, followed by multiple births and the dereliction of parental duty.

One evening, after Nol gave birth to another herd of abandoned foals, Father's skull was aching with all these thoughts. A pain emanated from deep in his guts, and he just wanted it gone. Without thinking, he started swimming. He swam further than he'd ever swum in one go before; he just kept going, without caring where he ended up. Looking back, he said it was a senseless thing to do – there were crabs and rays and so many other predators along the way, but it was the pain that pushed him on and powered his fins.

He kept going until he sensed a trembling in the water, a grumbling that shook his bones. And that's when he saw a volcano in the distance – the white smoke billowing – and he realised he'd reached Aberkariad. He'd been to Aberkariad once before with Uncle Nol, but he had detested the place: all the noise, the parading, the thrusting and the callous boasting and the pumping and the clicking – it had all seemed so indecent.

But now it was late, and Aberkariad was as quiet as a cave, and everything was still and empty, except for one horse who floated alone, her tail wrapped around seagrass.

Can't sleep? she said.

In the distance the volcano rumbled.

Not in ages, he replied.

Well, that makes two of us, she said.

At first, Father didn't know what to think of her. He sensed a certain coldness, but he also admired it: he liked that she hadn't immediately tried to mount him.

What's on your mind? she said.

The whirring in his head and the shuddering of the volcano all stirred inside of him.

I'm not doing well, he said.

The horse nodded and smiled.

You're not alone there, she said.

I am just so sick of pretending I'm fine, he said.

Me too, she said. Truth be told, I'm lonely.

This is it, he said. The loneliness. Where does it even come from?

I've been too scared to ever ask, she said.

They fell into a long silence, and then the horse proceeded to tell Father things she'd never told anyone else: about her birth, and how it had felt to watch her father swim away. She spoke of her childhood, of the lack she had carried inside ever since, and the throbbing ache that kept her up at night.

Father's blood rippled, his gills flittered. It was as if the horse's face was transforming with every word she uttered.

He confided that he too had felt the same feelings. Some days, he told her, the pain would continually stream through his body until it all became overwhelming – and his systems would just cut out and he would spend days at a time floating the through the waters, feeling nothing at all.

So much of my life feels unreal to me, he told her. It's as if I'm watching it all happen to someone else.

They talked throughout the night and all through the morning, and when day broke, Father's tail began to glow, and he told the horse how it felt like he was finally commencing his life proper now. For so long, he'd just been swimming in circles, but now he could see his true course – and it was beautiful.

He told her how he'd felt the light inside of him throb since they had spoken their first words to one another, and she observed how his skin was indeed brightening, changing from light orange to red.

For the first time ever, his fins felt at rest.

It was hard to explain, he told us, but with this horse everything felt familiar and nostalgic, as if the present was a fond memory he wanted to always recall. It was the joy and blood-thrill of being understood, of being ready to give himself entirely to another.

When he explained all this to the horse, and told her how his inner light shone for her and only her, she kissed him.

'Oh!' our father exclaimed to us. 'Your mother and I were head over tails in love!'

On the mornings of their courtship, she greeted him by rubbing her snout against his. For their pre-dawn dance, they joined tails and promenaded around one another for hours, her eyes fixed on his, his eyes fixed on hers. Sometimes they even did the cha-cha.

Mother apparently adored silly jokes, and she was forever making up ridiculous dance moves to get Father to laugh. His own favourite was the one she called The Hurricane – she'd fill her bladder with gas and speedily zip upwards through the water, pretending she was being cast away by crazy winds. She, in turn, couldn't get enough of Father's impressions. She particularly loved his one of the carp who'd eaten something disgusting and couldn't get the taste out of its mouth. He told us that she made him do it repeatedly, her head flipping back as she succumbed to fits of laughter. Sometimes she'd laugh so much she would blush, and she would turn her back on Father while she composed herself. With her back to him, he would look at the distinctive red stripes that lined her dorsal and think how wondrous it was to be alive.

Other females would return to their territory after mating dances, but Mother stayed on. She and Father talked for hours about their plans for the future – and the sacred life-bond they were swearing to keep. They both despised the neglect and the selfishness they saw all around them. Neither wanted to be like the other horses, the ones who gave birth then left their fry to fend for themselves. Instead, they were passionate about setting up a family unit, raising their offspring together, and teaching the next generation how to survive and lead meaningful lives.

Some days they didn't need to talk. They just floated together quietly, their tails wrapped around the same reed, each content to be in the other's company. If she was tired and needed a little rest, he would keep watch for predators. And she, in turn, would do the same for him.

When Father fell pregnant with us, Mother visited each day, checking up and making extensive enquiries about his well-being. Was he eating enough? Was he comfortable? Did he want her to scratch his back with her snout? As the pregnancy progressed and he slowly brightened to match the bright red kelp they swung among, Father's pouch swelled. He felt buoyant with love – this shape-shifting, transformative force he was already feeling for the family they were forging together.

Snaffling at meals, he would listen contentedly as Mother sung merry songs about the future. In her songs, she and Father were raising a big family, and they all lived together, and they all looked out for each other, and no one felt as if they were travelling through the waters of life alone and unknown, drifting through the sea without hope or purpose.

Then one morning, a week before he was due to give birth, Mother didn't show up for their courting dance. Father waited all day, and only hunted nearby in case he'd miss her, but she didn't come. This worried him immediately – it was so out of character for her – but he figured she must have had a good reason. He knew for sure that she was still alive – he could sense it in his gills – and he was certain that she would soon return.

The following morning he woke early, though he hadn't

really slept at all. He hung onto the reeds in their usual spot, and he waited. He waited all day again, and he waited all night. And he waited the entirety of the next day, and the one after that. But she never showed.

It must have been because of the seasons, our father concluded. The skies above were darkening and the waters were becoming rough. It would have been too dangerous for her to visit.

He considered going to find her, but his brood pouch was stretching, bulging, as we all began to hatch and swim around inside him, jostling to be the first ones out into the world. He was close to bursting and he needed to conserve energy, so he decided to stay put.

Five tides later, alone and afraid, he went into contractions and thought he saw Mother peering at him from behind a rock, but it was only a hallucination, the delirium of birthing pain.

Because then, a moment later, it began: he thrusted and he expelled sixty, seventy tiny horses into the sea. He tried to gather the fry together, but they kept swimming off in all directions. His blood ran cold and his skin turned grey, but there was no time to think. Another surge came, and another gush of foals sprung forth out of his reach. And so it went. Each time he managed to gather a couple of small fry by his side and re-compose himself, another batch would be expelled from his pouch – another school of tiny horses flung out into the world confused and alone, swept away by the unforgiving tide. 'Come here!' he shouted to them. 'I'm your father and I love you.'

He said it was just too difficult, too tiring, to gather them and bring them all together in one place. It was an impossible task to achieve on his own.

In total he gave birth to over one thousand horses, almost all of whom were lost to the sea.

He told us: 'You six boys are the only ones who survived.'

'But your mother can't wait to meet you,' Father said.

And she'd be back any tide now, he just knew it, he could feel it.

I took the story on as though it were my own: in my bones, I felt Father's love, his loss, and his separation from Mother. I can't be sure, because I never talked about it with them, but I don't believe my brothers experienced it like this. I don't know why – I don't understand how siblings can be so different to one another – and neither do I judge them for how they felt. It's just something I observed. They were respectful enough to stop speaking about Aberkariad in Father's presence, but I sensed that they were somehow able to elude the shadows of his pain in ways I never could.

Maybe I was just seeing things differently, but after hearing Father's story about Mother, I felt a change in his behaviour. There was a new urgency in the lessons he taught us. His voice took on a fresh intensity as he tried to rapidly impart everything he knew. On certain subjects, he constantly repeated himself. Again and again, he emphasised to us the value of rest. He explained that compared to other creatures, us horses are very poor swimmers. Because our fins are small we are prone to exhaustion. Every year, he said, thousands of horses die through simple overexertion. The amount of times my father stopped a speeding brother in his gallop! 'Slow down!' he'd yell. 'Where's the drought?'

A couple of days after the story, however, we woke to find Aled missing. It sent Father into a tailspin. ('If he means to break my heart, he's going the right way about it.') When Aled eventually returned and said he had only popped out to practise his length-swimming, Father gave him another lecture on the importance of not tiring oneself out.

'But I'm not you!' Aled snapped. 'I'm young, I've still got energy!'

'All I'm saying is you need to pace yourself,' Father answered. 'This goes for all of you. Because, believe it or not, you will get old, and you never know when you'll need to set your fins a-flutter. When it comes down to it, a bit of rest could be the difference between living your days out here in the water or ending up as a nice dessert in some giant tuna's belly.'

And so the tides passed: with small family bickerings as Father attempted to make us into 'real horses'.

Mornings, he would wake early to find us the best sea-grass to curl our tails around. When he found a good spot, he would come back and gently wake us and bring us out for hunting lessons. We'd stalk out, holding still in our hiding spots, watching the copepod as they floated passed.

'The trick is keeping steady,' he'd whisper. 'Let them come to you. These fellas are blind, but they detect movement in the water. You need to keep so, so still if you're going to catch them.'

We'd gently swill around the rocky seabed like this, waiting till Father gave us the signal. As soon as prey came our way, he would nod and make a clicking sound, and we'd swivel our heads, and huuuuuuu! – we sucked and slurped those fellas right up our snouts.

One time, after a good hunt, we were all laughing and recounting the best bits when we arrived home to find Uncle Nol lying languorously on Father's clam-shell couch. His face was bloated, and his brood pouch was large and swollen; he looked grotesque.

As we swam in, he began bobbing his head and singing, 'Up the duff, up the duff, guess who's up the duff?'

My brothers gasped.

'Can I rub my snout against it?' Llwyd asked.

'It would be an honour,' Uncle Nol said, and he pulled Llwyd close.

'It's amazing!' Llwyd said. 'I can feel them all in there! There must be a million fry inside you!'

Uncle Nol nodded to Father then. 'I don't suppose you want a feel, do you?'

Father rolled his eyes and shook his head in reply. I watched Father's eyes closely as they slowly took in the picture of Uncle Nol. I wondered what he was thinking, how he saw our uncle. But then Father's face broke into a resigned smile and he swam over and offered his tail to Nol to shake.

'Well, here we are again,' Father said, before proposing that Uncle Nol stay for a celebratory dinner.

That evening, as Father prepared shrimp in the kitchen, Uncle Nol brought me and my brothers out to the swing-bench in the garden.

'It's clear your father's not gonna tell you any of this,' Uncle Nol said. 'So I guess it falls to me.'

He inhaled a little air then – the better to show off his swelling pouch. The skin looked so tight I feared the pouch might burst.

'The first thing you need to know is that fillies come with the tide and leave with the tide. You got that, kids? I love your father, but he talks a lot of guff about all this – that we should be monogamous, and that we should mate for life, but let me tell you – it's crab shit. You can't trust a filly. When you're courting, they'll tell you every-thing you want to hear. They'll greet you every morning, have a little dance with you, grab your tail, tell you they love you, tell you there's no other horse they want to mate with, that this is a life-bond and they can't imagine living without you, and then before you know it, you're up the duff, swollen with a thousand of their sprogs, and they've gone. Two tides after you give birth, you go to find them, but where are they? They've swum off to shack up with some other horse on the other side of the volcano.'

I let out an involuntary snort.

'Trust me,' he added. 'I know what I'm talking about – I've been with a *lot* of fillies.'

I hated everything Uncle Nol was saying. But I could see that his pregnant state bestowed him – in the eyes of my brothers – a certain authority. They gazed at him with wide eyes and listened with a special intensity. His round pouch granted him a degree of practical wisdom that our father's thin frame seemed to lack. But looking at Uncle Nol's pouch, I kept imagining the thousand tiny horses inside of him. In one of our recent night-time conversations, when everyone else was asleep, Father had told me again about how so few young foals lived more than a single tide because of parental neglect; and looking at Nol's fat pouch now, the nature of life and death seemed strange and cruel to me. How arbitrary it was that I should have lived, while so many others had died. It was a thin line that divided the good from the bad, and it was a thin line that separated our pleasant ease of living from the sheer horror of abandonment and death.

'Now listen up, and listen clear,' Uncle Nol said. 'There's no one true partner for anyone. We're out here alone. You just need to go to Aberkariad, get your pouch filled, and move on. That's what life is about.'

I couldn't contain myself any longer.

'But what about love?' I said.

Uncle Nol looked at me, then gave a pitiful shake of the head. 'You're worse than your dad, you are.'

All my brothers laughed at that.

'Look,' Uncle Nol said. 'When you grow up, you might meet a stunning horse, a real big one. The kind that really gets your gills pulsing. You might think it's a *great* idea to form a bond with her or him for the mating season. I admit I have had these thoughts myself! And hey, that's okay to believe. It's called hope, it's what gets us through the waves. But at the end of the day, when the moon shines high above, love is codswallop. Once the mating season's over, it's kaput, *move on!* There's no use being like Old Captain Loveheart over there and getting hung up on *one* horse.'

As Uncle Nol spoke, I felt a tingling in my coronet. I looked to the kitchen, where Father's face appeared in the window. He was whistling the tune to 'The Wave of Love', and for a moment I felt pity for him – and then I became angry at Uncle Nol for making me feel this way towards my father. Watching him slowly move around the kitchen, his face seemed to dissolve, change, until it finally belonged to someone I didn't recognise. The face didn't look like my father's at all, but like the face of the crazy old horse I once saw beyond the green kelp, the one who dithered in circles, muttering about sharks. But when that horse in the kitchen looked up and saw me watching, he smiled at me – a small, tired smile – and in that face I again recognised my father, and I understood, perhaps for the first time, that he was deeply sad.

'Shrimp!' Nol was shouting. 'Bring out the shrimp!'

That night I dreamt uneasy dreams. I was at the bottom of the ocean, swimming in the dark among the debris of the dead: all the horses who had never made it, their spines and flesh rotting and decomposing in the ocean floor.

When I awoke, Aled was already up and about.

'I'm off out for some hunting practice,' he said. 'Wanna join?'

'Why are you practising so much?' I asked. Bits of the dream still clung to me and my flesh rippled with every image I recalled.

'I'm going to Aberkariad,' he said. 'And I'm going soon.'

'But we're not ready yet,' I said. 'You heard what Father thinks.'

'Dad's wrong,' Aled said.

'He's not,' I said.

'Of course, he is,' Aled said. 'He's just scared of losing us, that's what it's all about.'

'You're the one who's wrong,' I said.

'Berwyn's coming too,' he said, 'and Ieuan, and Hywel. Are you in or what?'

'When are you going?' I asked, gently, weakly.

'I talked about it with Uncle Nol last night,' Aled said. 'Nol says if Dad won't do it, then he'll happily take us to Aberkariad. Once he's given birth and recovered, he'll be good to go. In the meantime, he wants us practising our swimming. It's a long journey.'

'It's really not right,' I said. 'You shouldn't—'

'We have to live our own life,' Aled said.

'I know that,' I said, 'but—'

'Listen,' Aled said. 'Are you a horse or a shrimp?'

'I'm clearly a horse,' I replied.

He snapped his head at me. 'Well start acting like one.'

His words pierced me and I lowered my head, and then he added: 'Ah look, I just want my brother to be happy.'

'I am happy,' I protested.

'Are you sure?'

'Of course,' I said. 'Why wouldn't I be?'

With Uncle Nol pregnant, Father seemed to withdraw into himself. He became oblivious to Aled's plotting, and between hunts he would retire to the couch and paint more portraits of Mother. One evening, he asked me to pose for him so that he could perfect the dorsal stripe that she and I shared.

'She's going to get such a kick out of seeing your stripe,' he said. 'She'll give you such a big cwtch.'

I tried to keep the smile on my face, but the effort became wearing, and the colour soon began draining from my body.

'What's going on?' Father said. 'Are you alright? Are you getting enough rest?'

'I'm not tired,' I said.

'Then what's the matter?' he said. 'I'm your father, you can talk to me.'

I sighed and I hummed. And then finally I said: 'I've been thinking about Aberkariad.'

'Oh,' my father said, putting down his reed.

'Were you ever going to tell us about it?'

'Of course,' he said. 'But only in good time.'

'Okay,' I said.

'And now's not the time. Once the seasons change and your tails lengthen, it'll be different,' he said. 'You boys will have met your mother by then, and all of *this* will have been worth it.'

'She's coming back,' I said, almost to myself.

'She really is,' he said, and then he looked up at all the portraits of Mother that lined our shelves. 'She's going to love you so much when she sees you. She loves you so much already. I hope you know that.'

'I do,' I said.

I joined my father in gazing up at the portraits, and for the first time in my life I realised that I doubted him.

Over the next week I shrivelled and my tail turned grey. I had an urge to flee, but I also felt a pressure – a physical pressure – to stay put. I felt finless and stuck. I was exhausted, as if some vital life force was seeping away.

One morning, I was hitched on a blade of grass outside our home when a sensation erupted through my body. It told me that I couldn't, shouldn't, swim even a tail's length away to the next blade of grass. If I left the spot I was in, if I so much as moved a single beat of my fins, terrible things would happen. I stayed there, stuck, for a long while, until Uncle Nol passed on by, singing an upbeat ditty, and I somehow came back to myself.

'Well hello there,' Nol said, looking slim and limber.

'How did it all go?' I asked, nodding at his empty pouch.

'Like a dream,' he answered, beaming. 'It was just: *ping ping ping, fry, fry fry.*'

'And where are they all now?' I asked, a current inside me beginning to rise.

'No idea,' he said, and he shrugged. 'It's none of my concern.'

The current inside of me rose higher still and my snout began to quiver.

'Don't look at me like that,' Uncle Nol said. 'This is how horses have always done things. We're *meant* to be independent. So please, don't go believing everything your crazy old father tells you.'

'Crazy?' I snapped. 'I'll tell you what's crazy: the fact that of all the horses ever born, fewer than one in two hundred ever survives into adulthood. And why? Because their fathers don't stick around. They up and leave, and then the poor kids have to learn everything on their own. Horses like you make me want to never have kids.'

'Woah, now,' Uncle Nol said. 'You need to calm it there.'

'I'm only stating the truth.'

'You mean the truth as your father tells it.'

'Well, is he wrong?' I said.

'Your father's soft in the head,' he said.

'My father's a good horse,' I said, and I could hear the anger in my voice. 'He has honour and integrity, and that's a lot more than you have.'

Uncle Nol clicked in derision.

'You're a bright kid, son, you always have been. But you've got to use your own head. Have you ever wondered why your father stays around here, looking after you kids? Has it ever crossed your mind to consider why he hasn't moved on and found himself a new filly? Or for that matter, why he hasn't gone to find your mother?'

'Because she's coming back,' I shouted. 'As soon as the seasons change.'

'Boy,' he said, 'the seasons have changed twice since you were born, and where's your mam, hey?'

The current was up in my throat now. I was furious. 'She's coming back, you stupid blobfish.'

Uncle Nol shook his head.

I spat at him, more in desperation than anger, because I suddenly realised I no longer believed what I was saying.

Uncle Nol looked at me. His big open face was full of sympathy.

'Boy,' he said.

'She's not coming back, is she?' I said.

'No,' he answered.

'But why?'

'Listen,' Uncle Nol said. 'Once upon a time, a filly made a promise to a stud, because she wanted to screw. That's all it was. A phoney trade. But your father was always too much of a pipefish to see it.'

'Why are you telling me this?'

'Listen now. That filly doesn't give a shit about you or any of the many other fry she's had and will continue to have.'

'What do you mean, "continue to have"?'

'She basically lives in Aberkariad,' Uncle Nol replied. 'Go there if you don't believe me. You'll recognise her. Cos credit where credit's due, she looks exactly like your father's paintings.'

The conversation filled my body with sensations I didn't want. A heavy liquid settled in my gut, and slow trickles of it seeped through me throughout the day. There was a tightness in my gills and with each breath a jagged tooth stabbed me, made me think I might die. My brothers were laughing and joking, but I couldn't join in. I was folding in on myself.

The following morning, however, my own brood pouch emerged, and I couldn't be sure if all these sensations coursing through my body were because of the conversation or because of the pouch. I looked down at the pouch and was filled with disgust. I had lied to my body: I had led it to believe that I was ready to be an adult, but it felt absurd to me that a female could now drop her eggs into the pouch and within weeks I would be a father. All these young foals would enter the world; new lives, made without meaning or reason, except for the fact that two horses once had sex. The fry themselves would have no choice in the matter, in the same way I had never chosen to be chosen. It seemed incredible, almost negligent of nature, that there was nothing else governing this, that no greater permission need be sought. I realised then that anyone could become a parent – that what qualified you to have fry was not your intentions or your heart or your parenting abilities. You just had to be alive long enough and it would probably happen. And yet, this realisation didn't make me feel any more capable or up to the task. Deep down, I felt I still didn't measure up to some standard of fatherhood as I understood it. These ideas often took a physical shape: Father was still so much bigger than me, his tail so much thicker, his bones stronger, his voice deeper. But yet, it was more than just the physical differences that left me feeling ill-equipped. Father seemed, in unequivocal ways, archetypically adult. He possessed mental maps I could never read. How could my brothers even believe they were ready to become parents?

That afternoon, however, I joined Aled on a hunt, and I immediately saw how mistaken I was. In the last few weeks Aled had become astoundingly skilled at catching copepod, and I watched with awe as he sucked up meal after meal with such ease. He seemed to me like an adult.

'You're a different horse!' I said. 'You're fearless.'

'Well, I know what I want,' he said. 'And I know what I need. Once you know these things, everything else falls away.'

I didn't really understand. I had never before thought about what I wanted or what I needed. Surely I could only want what I needed. And Father had always been there to make sure we had all that we needed. So what more was there to want?

'How do you know what you want?' I said.

'Dad was right about the light,' Aled replied. 'You just have to be still a while, very still, and then you'll feel it.'

There was a silence between us. I tried to picture the light inside of me, but there was only a hole, a hole where the light should be.

'We're leaving tomorrow,' he finally said. 'Will you come with us?'

I let out an involuntary growl and turned my head. I didn't know if Nol had told him about Mother. I couldn't look at him.

'You can do whatever you like,' Aled said. 'It's your life. You've got the pouch now, you're an adult. But you have to make sure you're doing what *you* want to do. That's what Nol's always telling me.'

'I still think we should wait a bit longer,' I said. 'Then we can all go to Aberkariad together, you know? Father can take us, and Uncle Nol could maybe come along too. Why not wait a bit longer?'

'Cos I'm bored out of my skull.'

'You just need to keep patient. There's a season for everything.'

'Look, I'm not going to stop you doing whatever you need to do,' Aled said. 'But I'm done with being *told* what to do. I know what I want and I'm going to go get it.'

I sighed, realising that there was no convincing him.

'I'll miss you,' I said.

Aled smiled.

'Ah, but I'll be back before you know it,' he replied.

'Really?'

'Of course,' he said. 'I won't be gone for good. But let's go home now. I need some proper rest before tomorrow.'

And so we joined tails. As we glided home, I tried to really feel what it was I wanted. I brought my attention inwards, trying again to imagine the light. Was it firing? Was it dimming? If I did have a light inside of me, it felt as though it were aching.

When we reached the homestead, we detached from one another, and I thought of all the portraits inside the house. I pictured finally meeting Mother, and what I might say to her, and what she might say to me. I still didn't know if Uncle Nol had told Aled what he had told me. I considered saying something, but in the end I said nothing. I didn't want a big bust-up between Aled and Dad, not before Aled left. Or maybe I just didn't want to believe that Mother was in Aberkariad. Or maybe I was just being selfish, protecting myself. Or maybe I didn't want Aled to know that I already knew. It was easier to play dumb and just stay by Father's side. The more I think about it all now, the more I doubt if we can ever really know why we do one thing rather than another.

We were about to go inside when I saw a figure approaching us.

'Who's that?' I said.

'It's a filly!' Aled cried.

He was right. Apart from paintings I had seen so few fillies in real life that it felt uncanny for one to be so near. When she swam up close, I was struck by her wondrous eyelashes and her snout that was so beautifully curved.

'Well, well, well,' the filly said. 'You two must be Gareth's sons. I'd recognise those eyes in any waters.'

I smiled and nodded, and Aled inflated his brood pouch.

'*Adult* sons,' he confirmed.

'Duly noted,' the filly replied. 'Hey, your Uncle Nol said I might catch your father around these parts. Is he around? I'd love to have a little chat with him.'

'He's probably having a nap,' Aled said. 'But I can fetch him if you like?'

'There's a good boy,' she said. 'Thank you.'

'Just wait here,' he said. 'I'll be back before you know it.'

While Aled went to get Father, I stayed out front. In the filly's company, I became aware of my brood pouch and how it silently rested there between us.

'Nice day, isn't it?' she said.

I couldn't quite make eye contact with her. I kept thinking of my pouch and how it would feel full of eggs.

'Yes,' I said. 'Lovely day.'

I finally raised my eyes. The filly's rounded cheeks glowed, and her long snout seemed wise.

'We're old friends, your father and I,' the filly said, and I noticed how large her eyes were.

'Oh right,' I said.

She smiled. 'It's just I ran into your uncle recently and he mentioned your father. It got me wondering how he was doing.'

I didn't know what to say; in this filly's company, I felt strangely deferential.

'You know,' she said, 'you really do have your mother's snout.'

A cold tide surged through my body, but before I could reply, Father had joined us outside, with Aled beaming beside him.

When Father saw who it was, he told us boys to go inside for a minute.

'Who do you think she is?' Aled said when we reached the living room.

'She could be anyone,' I said, still thinking about Mother.

'Well obviously,' Aled said. 'She was sexy, though, wasn't she?'

'I don't know,' I said. I didn't know how you were meant to tell who was sexy and who wasn't. Had the filly thought I was sexy?

Father soon returned, panting and annoyed.

'Your bloody uncle,' he said.

'Who is she?' Aled said. 'Is she still out there?'

'He's an interfering humphead is what he is.'

We both stared at our father.

'Her name's Rhiannon,' Father said. 'She's someone I knew a long time ago.'

'Does she want to mate?' Aled asked.

'I'm too old and too tired for all that,' Father said. 'Once you bring up six boys, the thought of having any more is enough to make you want to lie down. Besides, I love your mother, and she'll be here soon.'

'Just as soon as the seasons change,' Aled scoffed.

'Exactly,' Father replied, as if he heard only the words and not the tone. 'Once the waters calm down, your mother will return and we can finally be a family again.'

Early the following morning, as Father slept on, we all waited outside for Uncle Nol's arrival. Aled entertained us with the mating dance moves he'd been busy practising all night, but the other boys seemed tense, quiet. Aled tried to gee them up, but it was obvious that something wasn't right.

Nol arrived, calling out, 'Ready, boys?' but only Aled answered, giddily yelling: 'Bring on the fillies!'

'Shh,' said Berwyn, 'you might wake Dad.'

'Good point,' said Uncle Nol. 'We don't want this to be any harder than it needs to be. Let's get going, is it?'

He unhitched himself, and began to swim away. But my brothers stayed still.

'What's going on?' Aled said.

'Well, the thing is, I've actually got this pain in my

head,' Berwyn said. 'I don't know if I should . . . you know. I want to, but I don't think . . . you know?'

'Oh right,' said Aled. 'I see. Well, how about you Ieuan?'

Ieuan's face was twisted with worry. 'My fin hasn't been right since that big hunt last week.' He shifted awkwardly. 'I think I might have strained it or something?'

Aled shook his head.

I could see Hywel almost shrinking, retreating behind us all.

'Howie, baby,' Aled said. 'Talk to me! How are we doing?'

But Hywel couldn't even speak. His face was shaking and his eyes kept moving in different directions.

'Okay,' Aled said, and then he turned to Llwyd, whose face was grey. 'Woah Llwyd,' he said, 'you actually do look peaky. Did you eat bad larvae or something?'

Llwyd yawned and his cheeks looked drained of colour.

'I just *didn't* get a good sleep,' Llwyd said. 'I'm knackered. There's no way I can do that swim.'

'I see,' said Aled, and then he blew out his cheeks.

Uncle Nol called out then, 'Are you boys coming or what?'

Aled looked dismayed. 'Boys, mun, this is what we've been waiting for.'

But in reply, our brothers only mumbled.

Aled turned to me then. 'Is it even worth asking you?'

'I don't want to go,' I said.

'Well, finally,' Aled said. 'Someone with the guts to just tell the truth.'

All my brothers bowed their heads.

'Look, I'm not going to make a scene here,' Aled said. 'But at some point you're all going to have to make your own way in this sea. We can't all keep following Dad.'

The boys nodded in unison.

'Come on,' Uncle Nol shouted again. 'Are we going or what?'

'Coming now!' Aled shouted in reply.

And then to us, he said: 'Well my brothers, the next time you see me, I guess I'll be pregnant. With a bit of luck, I'll be fat as a whale!'

We wished him all the best, and I urged him to stay safe.

Aled smiled, then turned away, me and my brothers waving our tails in goodbye.

As Aled and Uncle Nol swam away, growing smaller in the distance, I felt the light – I felt it so deeply – the light inside of me. It was weak and it was withering.

A day passed.

Then two days passed.

Then a week passed.

But neither Aled nor Uncle Nol returned.

I swam around with my brothers, and I hunted and I slept, but life seemed empty without Aled among us.

At night, Father and I stayed up talking. Father said that Aled had always been headstrong. In the end, he said, Aled always did whatever Aled wanted to do. Father was trying to act as if his leaving had no effect on him, but I began to see a certain pensive strain in his portraits of Mother. She seemed smaller, further away. She was still smiling in the paintings, but her lips were thinner and her smiles were more ambiguous, the waters around her darker.

As the days passed, I thought a lot about Aled. I imagined him returning pregnant and the dinner that Father would throw in his honour. I imagined him sat out on the garden swing-bench, telling us all about his travels. I would take strength from his experiences. Being close to him, I would absorb a little of his capabilities and begin to understand what I wanted or needed.

Some two weeks after they left, Uncle Nol returned. He came into the living room while Father was painting a portrait of Mother, once more studying my back so he could perfect the red stripe on her dorsal.

'Evening!' Uncle Nol called, showing off his pouch. He was pregnant again.

'Where's Aled?' I asked.

'Ah,' Nol said. 'Now here's the thing: your brother appears to have been struck down with Aberkariad fever.'

'What?'

'It can happen,' Uncle Nol said. 'Especially on first outings. I've seen it a hundred times before. A horse makes the trip, meets a young filly and their head swells with all these crazy ideas about love. It might be a while till you see your brother.'

'Wait, wait, wait,' Father said. 'What are we actually talking about here?'

'I think you know what I'm talking about,' Uncle Nol said and there was a bite in his voice. 'You know yourself the kind of horses you can meet out there.'

Father's eyes began to cloud. 'I told you he was too young to go,' he said. 'How many times did I say that, Nol?'

Uncle Nol blew out his cheeks. 'He was going to have to grow up at some point.'

'You're a piece of effin' crap shit,' Father said.

I had never before heard my father swear.

Uncle Nol went to reply, but Father shouted, 'I don't want to hear it,' and then he left the room.

Uncle Nol looked at me. 'What?' he said.

'I'm missing something here,' I said.

'Yeah, working testes,' he replied.

'Bugger off,' I said. 'What's going on? What's happened?'

'You really want to know?'

'Of course,' I said. 'Aled is my brother.'

'Well young boy, your *brother* has just met your *mother*.'

'What?'

'I told you she was at Aberkariad. I wasn't lying. Your brother met her and—'

'Aled met our mother,' I said, before even realising I had said it out loud.

'Yes, your mother. And . . . well . . . the conversation didn't end well, and now he's flung himself at the nearest filly; and, if truth be told, he's not right in the noggin. I haven't seen anyone this bad since your father.'

My mind was a shoal of questions, each one bustling the other out of the way. I couldn't quell the tumult, but I knew I had to act before I froze.

'We have to go back then,' I said. 'We have to help him.'

'I don't know if you can help a horse like that,' Uncle Nol replied.

I looked at Uncle Nol's swollen face, the way his eye-spines seemed to have retreated into his head.

'Do you even care about Aled?' I said.

'What a stupid question,' he said. 'Of course I do. But I went through all this with your father once before. I went to Aberkariad and I dragged him back, and a fat lot of good that did.'

I felt the colour draining from my skin and I realised what I had to do.

As the evening darkened, my insides wound and knotted like weeds. There was a heaviness in my bladder, and it kept tightening and tightening until I approached Father. Once more he was perched on the clam-shell couch, painting another portrait of Mother. In the portrait her tail was gripping the leaf of a blue kelp, her back to the viewer.

'I think I should go and get Aled,' I said.

Father didn't look up. It was as if he couldn't make eye contact.

'Okay,' he said, and I watched him apply brushstrokes

to the painting. In the portrait the water was so dark it was almost black.

'I'm worried about him,' I said.

Father finally looked up at me.

'You know, son,' he said, 'you're a good horse. You'll make your mother very proud.'

Uncle Nol had explained the route, but I still wasn't confident of the way. I couldn't keep in mind the order of the seamarks. In some stages, the waters hummed with life, with schools of flame cardinals and blackcap basslets. When puffers and jellies passed by, I obscured myself, as father had taught me, blending into the nearest grass.

But swimming on, the waters grew darker and I could barely see a tail's breadth ahead of me. After a while, I was no longer able to distinguish between weeds and fronds. The currents kept pushing me off course. Father had been right: we weren't ready to make this trip. Swimming against the tide, my tail felt too short, and my fin too small. It became a gruelling effort to just keep going.

I was exhausted, so I took a break among the grass. I fed on copepod and tried to regather my strength. My bones were as heavy as rocks and my body felt as old as time. But I had swum too far to turn back. Hitched there, I realised how small and inconsequential I was, that all my life I had just been this tiny light moving through a limitless expanse of dark. I turned the thought over, picturing the image of the light in the dark, and soon the thought humbled me, and I felt oddly reassured. My brother was far away, and between us was all kinds of danger, but I knew that if I just kept going, kept focusing on the beating of my fins, on moving one small increment at a time, I could reach him.

I let go of the grass. At first, my fins burned with the struggle, but I dropped deep inside of myself and heard a voice within – a whisper – telling me that I could do it. Moving at a steady pace, I chanted a silent spell:

A-ber-kar-iad
A-ber-kar-iad
A-ber-kar-iad

Each syllable was a stroke of my fins, and each syllable, I knew, would bring me to my brother. As I swam, the water no longer seemed to work against me. I was in harmony with it.

Onwards I swam, my head no longer a heavy weight. Not one restricting thought could hold me back. I quickened my chanting – *A-ber-kar-iad, A-ber-kar-iad, A-ber-kar-iad* – and I quickened my stroke, and my body and mind were as one, and I moved through the water, not with ease as such, but with a firmness of intention. I was finally sure of what I wanted and it was glorious and easy, this wholeness of being. I was thinking all these thoughts and feeling all these feelings, blinded really, when I saw the eel, its gaping mouth ready to swallow me whole.

It was all about to end – my history and future – extinguished in one bite; the light inside of me forever dimmed in the belly of an eel, but what's strange, and what I've never told anyone, is this: in that moment, I felt ready. Maybe it was just fear, or maybe it was another feeling, a feeling I won't let myself understand, but I accepted my fate and took one last breath – and then I felt a tugging in my tail, and the eel swam on by as I was pulled into a forest of grass.

'Bloody hell,' Rhiannon said. 'In the mood for a bit of dying are you?'

I shook my head.

'Where are you trying to go?' she said. 'Because if you're trying to get home, I can assure you that an eel's stomach is not a shortcut.'

'Aberkariad,' I said. 'My brother – I have to find him.'

'Duw duw, you really are your father's son,' she said. 'Hitch up, and I'll lead the way.'

With nothing left inside of me, I clutched my tail around Rhiannon's. I was anxious at first, and I kept seeing the image of the eel whose mouth I'd only marginally escaped. But as we moved steadily through the water it felt good to be holding her tail, and I gradually began to feel calm, serene even. I was sleepy still, but I was alive, and for that, the world was a beautiful place. A sensation of warmth spread through my entire body. Though when the warmth reached my crown, I began seeing images of what lay ahead, and the warmth became a prickly heat, and my gills tremored. Because it dawned on me now: that very soon I would finally meet my mother.

Rhiannon said she needed a breather, so we stopped to feed on plankton. In the distance I saw a volcano pumping out smoke.

'Is that Aberkariad?'

'It is,' she said. 'Well, not the volcano itself, but the waters around it.'

'Is it a big place?'

'It can seem both large and small,' she said. 'Right now, with all the horses there, it's a metropolis. But later on, when it empties out, it can feel a very quiet place indeed.'

'I hope Aled is okay,' I said. 'Will he be easy to find?'

'There's no knowing,' she said.

I sighed and clicked.

'I hate this,' I said.

'Hate what?'

'Not knowing anything. I thought once I got a brood pouch, I'd just *understand* things. But I don't. I know I'm technically an adult, but I still don't feel like one, not the way Aled does.'

Rhiannon laughed.

'I bet your brother is as confused as you right now,' she said. 'Becoming an adult doesn't magically make you any smarter or wiser. I'm sure even your father feels out of his depth sometimes. I know I do.'

I looked at Rhiannon now, at her elegant snout.

'How exactly do you know my father?'

She paused.

'He didn't tell you?'

'No.'

'Well, we have some . . . history.'

'What does that mean?'

'If he hasn't spoken to you about it, then—'

'Please,' I said, and I heard the exasperation in my own voice.

She puckered her mouth and clicked.

'We mated once,' she said.

Every part of me felt still.

'My father has had other foals?' I said.

'Of course,' she said. 'You didn't know?'

'No,' I said.

'Oh shit,' she said. 'I'm so sorry.'

The volcano burped out a cloud of gas, and it was as if the gas moved through my gut, my gills, my bladder. I had no words now; I was just a body full of churning, like the seabed after a commotion, the dust and dirt swirling.

'This was years ago,' she said. 'We were both very young at the time. We were just starting out. The same age as you are now. It was long before your father met your mother. I think that's why he's so protective of you boys. He wanted to put things right.'

I remained motionless. All the air had left my body.

'Look,' she said. 'That's all in the past now. He loves you boys to bits.'

'I don't understand,' I said.

'Don't tell him I told you,' she said. 'If he kept it secret, he obviously had his reasons.'

I pictured all these other fry, all these foals, my brothers and sisters, all floating in the deep waters, all alone and afraid.

'Are you okay?' she said.

'I don't really know what I think,' I said.

'Ah,' she said. 'Maybe you are an adult after all.'

We swam on then, until directly ahead of us was the volcano. It was belching giant bubbles and clouds of gas. Lit in its eerie light, the waters of Aberkariad twinkled and shimmered. I swam alongside Rhiannon, the sea ahead of us crackling with horses twirling coloured circles around one another. I heard the pulsing and the writhing, and the frenzy of clicking and growling as males pumped their pouches, and females tried to hitch onto them to mate. The waters around us vibrated, and my gills shook as the clicking grew louder.

I tried hard to focus both my eyes. The waters glittered: green, orange, red, the whole scene dancing in light.

'What are all those colours?' I asked as we neared.

'It's incredible, isn't it?' Rhiannon said, and her small mouth broke into a smile. 'That's mating in action. Horses changing skin colours to flirt. Some horses brighten to stand out from the crowd, while others transform to match their partners. It makes for quite a dazzling sight, doesn't it? Every time I'm here, it takes my breath away.'

I was stunned by the spectacle and couldn't imagine

myself being among it all.

'There's just so many horses,' I said. 'How will I ever find my brother?'

'You're determined,' she said. 'That part is obvious. And when you're determined, you can go a very long way. You might surprise yourself yet.' She smiled and unhitched her tail from the grass.

'Are you leaving me now?' I said.

'It's probably best we say goodbye here,' she said. 'Once you get in there, it can get kind of crazy.'

'Where are you going?'

'I'm meeting an old partner,' she said. 'We've been meeting regularly for a while now.'

'So some horses do stay together?'

'Some do, some don't,' she said. 'But you never know how it's going to go.'

I laughed without really knowing why.

'Ah, there's those eyes again,' she said. 'Do me a favour: when you see your father next, please don't be too rough on him. He's a sweetheart, really.'

I pictured my father at home. At this moment he was probably resting on the couch, painting another portrait, waiting for me and Aled to return.

O Aberkariad! There were just so many heaving bodies, promenading around one another, touching snouts, clicking and pumping. After the smallness of my family, it was unreal to be among the throng of a city. From a distance, the horses had all seemed on top of each other, but moving through them now, I saw there was order, though I didn't really understand the rules. As I swam through, male horses shouldered me out of the way, shouting at me for swimming in the wrong channels. Was I an idiot? they asked. Was there something wrong with me? I apologised, tried explaining that I was new here, that I was just looking for my brother, but they scoffed and told me they weren't interested in my life story, and could I please just get the fuck out of the way.

Everywhere I looked, there were short snouts, long snouts, tails twice my length, and skin colours that sharpened and brightened as bodies neared.

A blue filly with large eyes approached.

'You're a cute one,' she said. 'Would you like to dance?'

But I said no, I wasn't that kind of horse, and that I was only looking for my brother.

She laughed and moved on to another horse beside me, a young stud whose brood pouch swelled in readiness.

The waters around us were quivering with desire, but to my eyes there was very little of what Father had told us about love.

I swam and I swam, and I called out my brother's name, the strobing colours leaving my eyes dizzy, and the clicking and pumping of pouches becoming a sore rhythm in my head.

I saw males pursuing females, and females escaping the clutches of drawn-out tails. I saw females butting heads with males. I saw males tail-wrestling rivals out of the way, the females looking on, almost bored by it all. I saw copulation and kissing, and stroking and caressing, but I just kept moving.

Exhausted, I finally rested in an empty patch of grass on the far side of Aberkariad. It was, thankfully, unpopulated, and I was the only horse hitched there, though I could still hear the nearby moans of mating couples. Their pulsing trembled through me, so I tried to focus on the swaying grass and cast aside the image of all those horses. But my thinking kept looping back to them, and to thoughts of Uncle Nol. Why did he always come here? Why did he always want to be pregnant? Was it a want or a need? When Aled had talked about wants and needs, I couldn't see the difference between the two. Watching the grass sway, I became almost hypnotised by the questions: what did I want? What did I need? I'd never before regarded myself as existing separately from my brothers. There was Father and there was us boys. We did as he told us, and I felt as he felt.

Through the twitching blades of grass, then, an older filly emerged, the green leaves parting as she passed between them.

'Well hello there,' she said.

'Hi,' I said.

'You look deep in thought,' she said.

'I've come a long way,' I said.

'We all have,' she said and she smiled. 'Where are you from? Would you like to dance?'

'I'm not looking for a mate, sorry,' I said. 'I'm looking for my brother. Have you seen him? We have the same snout, and the same eyes, though he's a much better hunter and swimmer than I am.'

'There are a lot of horses around here,' she said. 'But if I do meet anyone matching your very thorough description, I'll tell him you're after him. Why do you need to find him?'

'He's apparently gone a bit mad,' I said.

'Oh,' she said. 'Yes, I've definitely seen that happen before.'

I nodded as if I understood.

'But look,' she said. 'I'm not after a screw. I just thought it could be good to dance. Do you like dancing?'

'I need to find my brother,' I said.

'Wherever he is, I doubt he's leaving any time soon. So take it from me: have a break. You need to dance. Because right now, you look so tense. A good dance will help you relax. I swear by it.'

Against my conscious will, her words stirred inside me; maybe I didn't want to dance, but a dance was what I needed?

She said: 'Have you ever danced with a filly before?'

'No,' I said. 'But I did hold tails with one earlier.'

'Ah, so you're halfway there already,' she said. 'This will be easy for you, and an honour for me.'

She moved in close then, as close as she could be without touching. My guts whirled, and I felt my brood pouch becoming moist.

She was older than me, considerably, and her eyes looked tired, but there was no doubting she had once been beautiful. Her snout seemed almost familiar, as if all the other snouts I'd ever seen were based upon it.

'You have a lovely smile,' she said. 'And such lovely eyes.'

'Thank you,' I said.

'Shall we promenade?' she asked, and then she explained the moves.

As we danced and circled each other, a future unfolded within me. I felt it enacting a pull upon my fate. The filly drew near, bringing her snout so close to my face. I felt nervous and giddy. Suddenly, her tail was entwined in mine, and it felt good to be held like that.

'And promenade!' she said. She let go of my tail, turned 180, and then I saw her back, and the red stripe – so distinctive it was unmistakable from all the portraits I had spent my lifetime looking at.

I stopped dead. And yet she continued to spin around me.

'See, dancing isn't hard,' she said. 'You just have to let yourself go and feel the mood.'

She was smiling still. She began bobbing her head from side to side then, as if to make me laugh. Some essential part of me had left my body and I was hitched now to the spot.

Her mouth was twitching with a smile, and I watched as her expression shifted, flattened.

'What's wrong?' she said.

'I have to go,' I said.

'Wait,' she said.

'I have to go now.'

'What's wrong?' she said. 'What's happening?'

I did not answer. But when I turned to leave, I heard her gasp.

'Oh my gills,' she said.

I didn't know what to do then. I didn't know whether to turn around and face my mother, or swim into the waters of the nearest predator.

'Your brother,' she said. 'I spoke with him a few days back. He said there were more of you, and that one of you had my stripe. But I didn't believe him.'

I turned to face her now. She already looked different. Older, sadder.

'His name is Aled,' I said. 'And you drove him crazy.'

'My darling, I just told him the truth.'

'The truth?'

'I am so sorry,' she said. 'Please know I'm sorry.'

'Really?' I said. 'You're sorry are you? For what exactly?'

'For everything,' she said. 'For Aled, and for this, and . . . Your brother explained how much your father talked about me.'

'Well, if you're so sorry, then why didn't you ever come back?'

'I just couldn't,' she said. 'I didn't have – I didn't have it – I just didn't—'

'Didn't have what?'

'It's hard,' she said and her voice broke.

'What's hard?'

'It's hard to admit this. To admit to having these feelings.'

I looked at her.

'Why didn't you come back?' I said. 'You made a promise.'

She sighed, and I watched as her face crumpled.

She said: 'I just didn't – I just didn't feel I had enough love inside of me.'

Her words landed like a heavy stone in my gut. I was ready now to sink to the bottom of the ocean.

'Your father told me that love was a light that shined inside of him,' she said. 'Well, it didn't shine in me.'

'That's not what he told us.'

'I mean, I did have the light once,' she said. 'And it was with your father. When we met, I felt love glowing inside of me, and I thought: yes, this is it. I felt ready for the life we had talked about: a family, together, forever. But then, something changed. In my heart, summer became winter. I don't know how, and I don't know why. One day, I just looked at your father, and I felt nothing. And I knew then that I could never give myself to anyone else.'

'To no one?'

'Not to any male and not to any offspring,' she said. 'I know that I broke your father's heart when I told him I didn't love him. But I thought it was better to tell the truth than to live a lie.'

'So he knew you weren't coming back?'

'Of course,' she said. 'I told him before he gave birth. He's always known.'

'Then why didn't he tell us?'

'I don't know,' she said. 'I never realised he didn't.'

We both remained still, motionless in the water.

A large stud swam between us then. Looking at Mother, he said, 'Hey sweet thing. How about filling this big hole of mine, eh?'

She looked at him and shook her head.

'Come on baby, you know you want to,' he pleaded.

Mother looked at him.

'Would you just piss off?' she said, and the male pulled a face at me – as if to say, 'Fillies, eh?' – and then he swam on, without a care in the sea.

We were both quiet then. I looked up and I watched her sigh and cast her head down. I wondered how much of her was within me already. Would my feelings come and go like hers? I'd never felt the light within me fully, not really. Not the way Aled did, not the way my father did. Maybe I had no real light, maybe there was just an empty chamber where the light should be.

Slowly she raised her face to look at me. 'Are you okay?'

I went to answer, but then, without warning, a howling noise passed through my body and out of my mouth. I howled and I howled and my skin rippled, and everything was still; it was as if a deep ache was leaving my body. It was leaving me through the howl. The howl was coming from long ago, from long before me, but lived within me still, in the empty chambers whose walls echoed with the sounds of the howl.

'Oh boy,' she said, 'I'm so, so sorry.'

'Why though?' I said, and the why was a howl. 'Why did he lie?'

'I think I probably know why,' she said.

I was choking and all I could say was why and why and why.

Her face became a warm smile then, the same smile that all my life had shone down at me from the portraits.

And then my mother said: 'I think your father just wanted you to always feel loved. Is that such a bad thing?'

When I eventually found him, Aled's eyes were romping, and he was sucking on something that wasn't there. He looked thin, as if he hadn't been eating properly.

'My earnest brother!' he said, laughing. 'Come to disapprove, have you?'

'I've come to bring you home,' I said.

'Ah, a wasted journey then,' he replied, and he started telling me his story. He spoke quickly, his sentences frantic. From what I could understand, he had fallen in love with a filly named Susan from the other side of the volcano. They had been dancing together for days now, but she was, for some reason, reluctant to mate. When I pressed him to explain, he started talking about the volcano.

'It's the heart of everything,' he said. 'I don't know what it's pumping out but I can't get enough of it. Maybe it's love it's pumping out. Maybe I need to get Susan into the volcano.'

'Where is she?' I said.

'She's gone back to her side of the water. I keep visiting, but her sisters tell me to leave and just wait for her. So that's what I'm doing. I'm not leaving here until I've waited for her. I think I'm maybe too small for her, maybe that's what it is. I just need to wait here until I'm fully grown, and maybe then I'll be enough.'

'What are you talking about?' I said. 'You're more than enough. You're a great horse.'

'Really?' he said. 'Well, if I'm so great, why doesn't Susan love me?'

His eyes were restless, darting in all directions. Looking at him, everything fell away: I saw through this adult shell of his – I saw the little colt in him.

'Is this about Mother?' I said. 'What did you two talk about?'

He fidgeted, sucked again on something not there.

'Dunno what you're on about,' he said, and he started nodding his head quickly.

'You met Mother,' I said.

'Oh, I've met a lot of crazy old fillies out here,' he said, and then he blew out his cheeks and inflated his brood pouch. 'But I'm my own mam now. The volcano is my mam. Love is my mam. Maybe Susan is my mam. You can be my mam if you want.'

He laughed then.

'We'd need to get you into the volcano first!' he said,

and then he continued to laugh to himself.

'You have to come home,' I said. 'Come back with me. You'll be able to rest, eat properly, and get a good sleep. In a few days, you'll feel yourself again, I promise.'

'But I feel great!' he said, and he burst upwards, until he was high above. And then just as quick, he swooped back down beside me. 'I'm alive!' he cried. 'I'm feeling everything, I'm open and everything is flowing through me. I'm lit from head to tail. Can't you see that?'

'Please,' I said. 'Please come home. I'm worried about you, Aled.'

'That's Dad's doing,' he said and he chuckled to himself. 'You've taken on his worry as your own. But look into that volcano – really look into it! – and let it fill you. Some days, I just stare at it, and I watch the bubbles rising and each bubble is like a new thought, and it allows me to see everything with new eyes. That's what love is, I promise. It's new eyes.'

He smiled then. 'You don't understand me, do you? You don't understand what I'm saying?'

'I don't know,' I said.

'You have to learn to see things for yourself,' he said. 'Otherwise, what are you actually looking at?'

Aled wouldn't budge. I pleaded and I begged, but he would not leave, so in the end I left without him.

It took me two days to get home.

On the evening I returned, the homestead from outside seemed so small. After all my travels, it was faintly astonishing that the house could still be there, that my father could still be inside. It felt unnatural, like revisiting a day from the past.

That night, as hard as I tried, I couldn't sleep. When I came down for a bite to eat, I found Father perched on the clam-shell couch, painting another portrait of Mother.

He looked up at me. 'She really was a beauty.'

'Dad—' I said.

'She's coming back,' he said. 'She told me she would. She made a promise.'

'You can move on now,' I said. 'We're old enough now. You can leave here, do whatever you want.'

'But your mother—'

'She's not coming back,' I said. 'You don't have to pretend for my sake.'

'I'm not,' he said. 'Your mother loves you and she'll be here any time now. As soon as summer comes, she'll be back.'

Time passed, waters warmed and cooled then warmed again, and I forgave my father without ever telling him I knew the truth. Though maybe it wasn't true forgiveness, maybe it was just cowardice on my part and I was just avoiding a fight. Maybe I don't know the meaning of forgiveness. Maybe instead of forgiving my father, I buried the pain deep down, and that's what aches at night. I do sometimes wonder if his lies about Mother are what damaged me most. If I had never expected her love, would I have ever felt its loss?

Against my will, I noticed Father becoming greyer around the eyes, I noticed how his tail lost colour, how his speech slowed, and how he began to forget what he was talking about and would break off, then repeat himself. He began sleeping more; he started taking naps in the day while the boys and I went out hunting. He ate less and I watched him, day by day, shrivel and shrink before me. The frailer he became, the more my anger seemed inappropriate. In response to his demise, my feelings softened, muted.

By the time us boys would arrive home from our hunts, Father would be fast asleep on the couch, lying horizontal, his head resting on a rock, snoring not loudly, but not with grace. I don't know why, but the sight and the sound of him – his head on the rock, his small collection of shiny stones set in front of him – the whole thing made me terribly ashamed.

One by one, my brothers left for Aberkariad and not one of them returned to visit. By most accounts, they each fell pregnant, and each of them abandoned their fry. I haven't seen any of them in ages, though a turtle told me that Aled is dead – mad on love and loss, he went raging down a dark channel and was swallowed by a spotted eagle ray.

I was the last of the fry to leave home. It twists my guts to remember the day. When I told Father I was just popping out for an after-supper swim, he looked up from his painting and smiled.

'An after-supper swim,' he said. 'What a lovely thing to be able to do.'

I looked down at the portrait he was working on. It was uncanny – the bright grin, the pouch full to the brim – it was unmistakably Uncle Nol. The very same Uncle Nol who – Rhiannon had told me the day before – had passed away at Aberkariad, just as he'd always wished.

'It's a great likeness,' I said.

'Ah, it's alright,' my father answered. 'But a portrait is always a poor substitute for the real thing.'

His eyes were full of feeling, a feeling I knew all too well but could no longer carry with me. Father tried to brighten, but his smile was blue and fading. I knew for sure then that I had to leave. I felt it within me, the flame was withering, and I had to go before my father's sadness and kindness killed the light forever.

Because it was a kindness, what our father tried to give us. The story of our mother was a lie, but I believe he meant it as a gift.

When I think back on those early days of my life, I remember the colours of plants, and my childhood fascination with them, the way the very specific shade of red kelp meant something holy and mythic to me, and how I would have happily spent an entire day staring entranced at its swaying fronds. I remember how tired I'd be after swimming any distance. I remember my blood running cold when I saw a predator – and I remember the relief, and the sound of Aled's manic giggling when it swam on by. I remember the great size of everything, and the feeling that I was small in the world but saw things as they actually were, and how I thought I could handle anything that came my way. I remember how on a golden evening of hunting and laughing with my brothers, time would stretch and those evenings felt like forever. And on the coldest nights, I remember the warmth of being among my brothers, of the joy and the thrill of belonging to this sacred family, and the way that the light inside of me was fanned by the glowing embers of our father's love.

Sometime after leaving my father, I began meeting regularly with Rhiannon. She was wonderful company, and for a while I thought she might close the gap I felt inside. We would often stay up late, talking about our lives, and she would listen with care and patience as I spilled my guts, as I tried to express my guilt and confusion at my father's life. At some level, I felt I was to blame for how things turned out for him. When I reflected on the smallness of his life, it made me wonder: what was it all for?

One night Rhiannon said to me: 'When you have children yourself, maybe you'll find that it's enough to live for them and them alone.'

'But how could we have ever been enough for him?' I asked. 'How could we have ever been enough, when we meant so little to her?'

I have yet to settle down myself. My friends say I am too fussy, that I am over-critical, but I tell them: I just haven't met the right horse yet, and there are still things I want to do before I become a father. There are things I want to understand.

But maybe I'm asking the wrong questions and I'm wondering the wrong thoughts. Maybe, by the end, my father didn't think about his life in terms of a purpose beyond his being a parent. Maybe in the end it just became a matter of getting through each day, of getting enough food to eat, and keeping the light burning – keeping all us kids alive and loved. But when I think about these things for too long, I do get down. I begin to see my own life in abstractions, and I begin to wonder what my own life means – and what any life is really for.

There's a hole in all of us, I believe. We can try to fill the hole with explanations and distractions, and for a while our efforts might work and we might go to sleep feeling full, but in the morning we'll always wake up empty. Though maybe I'm dressing all this up too profoundly, maybe I'm straining. Maybe the thing I can't get over is just the sad bare facts of it all: Mother never did return, and Father died alone.

Little Wizard

Look at this, Michelle said, wielding a sheet of A4 paper. Big Mike reached for his reading glasses, a gesture that always seemed to him quite professional. Looking over the page, he thought he recalled collating the figures a few months back. Michelle was watching him closely, and he wondered how long was a normal length of time to look at the sheet. She was always complaining that he worked too slowly, so he didn't want to take ages over it. But she also often told him he was never thorough enough, so he didn't want to look up too soon. He stroked his day-old stubble and made a concentrating noise, hoping it didn't sound affected.

Okay, he finally said. What now?

Nothing strikes you as . . . odd? she said.

He looked again at the print-out. Dates, sums, clients. He normally used Arial for stuff like this. Maybe he hadn't put the sheet together after all.

What font is that? he said.

It's not about the font, Michael. Look at the actual content. Do you see anything strange there?

He looked down at the sheet.

I dunno, he said.

What do you mean, you don't know? You either think there's something odd or you don't.

Okay then, I don't see anything odd there. Alright?

Fine then, she said. There is nothing odd with this Reconciliation that you put together. I can send it off to accounts, and not be worried at all. Is that what you're saying?

Well, I dunno now.

Why don't you know?

Because you're making me think there might be something wrong with it.

Am I making you think there's something wrong, or is there something wrong with it?

That's what I'm asking. Can you give me a hint?

It's not a pub quiz, Michael.

Do you want me to open the file on the computer, then?

If it's not too much of a bother.

I'm sorry, he said.

Somewhere in there is a catastrophic mistake, she said. And you made it.

Okay, he said. I'm sorry. I'll sort it now.

Stop saying sorry, she said. I just want you to concentrate on your job. I'm not asking for too much.

She dragged her chair over, then sat behind him while he searched through folders on his desktop. When he double-clicked the Reconciliations file, Excel was slow to load, and Michelle sighed. He hated her sighs. He'd have preferred for her to punch him in the face instead of sighing. Every huff flooded his blood with dread, reducing him to something very small. There'd been times when he had sat frozen at his desk, long after five-thirty, because her sighs had made him afraid to do or say anything. Tracing his fingers across the rows and down the columns now, a tightness spread through his shoulders. He re-input figures, but under Michelle's surveillance he kept making typos. At one point she openly snorted.

After forty minutes he found the mistake: a misplaced decimal which made everything wrong.

Be honest with me, Michael, she said, are you trying to lose your job?

Of course not, he said, but Michelle just shook her head and went back to her desk.

He waited a few minutes, pretending to concentrate on emails, and then he got up, went to the toilet and locked himself in the cubicle. Sat there, staring at the grey stall door, his leg began shaking and he smelled bitter b.o. rising through his shirt. His armpits were so hot, and his face was burning, a heat rash spreading in his cheeks. He removed his reading glasses, the sweat trickling along his ears. He was aware now of his collar rubbing tightly, so he undid the top button, stroking the welt on the back of his neck. Taking out his phone, he set it to Camera and watched himself in the screen. The dark bags under his eyes were deeper than usual, he looked tired and swollen and miserable. But watching himself in the camera made the whole thing unreal – and the hand holding the phone didn't seem like his own. He studied the other hand, the one resting on his lap. He raised it to his face. No, it wasn't his hand at all.

The blue shirt he put on this morning was an alien shroud, designed to fool people into thinking he was a real person. He didn't know even where the real him was. He wasn't inside of himself any more. He watched his image in the screen again, the sorry eyes staring back. Whoever this person was, whoever had been going around pretending to be him, they were pathetic. He took a photo, to catch the imposter off-guard. The phone made the fake camera sound, and he stared at the freeze-frame image, then touched the screen to zoom in. Oh it was him alright, but the him that he hated.

He rested the phone in his lap, and dropped his face into his hands. There was no way out. He was stuck in his body, and his body was stuck in this cubicle, and there was nowhere for him to go. He began heaving, then found that he was wailing, a noise choking from the back of his throat. He was crying, but he didn't want Michelle to hear. He quickly took another photo of himself, and considered sending it to Rhian. It would be like evidence, or something. But he knew he couldn't actually show Rhian, because she told him once that she didn't like it when he was sad. It was the story of his life: he was always forced into being the funny one, offering himself up as the punchline to every joke. You always bring the fun, his mum once told him after making her laugh when she'd been crying at the kitchen table. He was ten at the time and he'd understood her remark to mean that he wasn't ever allowed to be anything but the fun-bringer. And it had been that way ever since: his friends only liked him when he was chirpy. Whenever he got drunk and ended up getting deep, or sad, or complaining about how it actually really sucked to be five-foot-three – no one wanted to hear.

When he returned to his desk, his eyes red, Michelle said she had to leave early and she asked that he send over the corrected file before he left. The mood was different now, as if they were coming down a hill, and she had realised that they both knew that she had gone too far. He nodded at her, and said, Yeah, no bother, and then she wished him a good evening and he said, You too. Through the window, he watched her drive away, then he went to YouTube and searched 'man utd bayern munich', and selected a seven-minute video of the 1999 Champions League Final, dragging the scrollbar to the last three minutes of the video, so that he could watch Teddy Sheringham swivelling to score, Alex Ferguson in his suit cheering, then Ole Gunnar Solskjær poking the ball into the roof of the net, and sliding on his knees, and Peter Schmeichel cartwheeling, the commentator's voice breaking. He watched the goals a couple of times each, then logged off and left the office.

Driving home, his body felt hollow. He called into the Tesco in Penyrheol and picked up a pepperoni oven pizza, a box of Dairy Milk chocolate fingers, and a two-litre bottle of Coke. At the self-checkout he scanned the pizza, but the machine told him there was an unexpected item in the baggage area. He took the pizza out and tried to put it back, and the message came up again. This happened a few more times until the woman in the machine lost patience and said, Help is coming, but when he looked around there was just a bald man in the queue looking at him.

He turned back to the machine. Above the check-out his own face was in the security screen, the colour washed out.

A staff member approached then, a woman in her fifties wearing the blue polo shirt.

Sorry, Big Mike said. I dunno what I've done wrong.

Oh don't worry love, the woman said. It's not your fault. She's a fussy cow, she never shuts up. I can literally hear her when I'm sleeping.

Big Mike laughed, and the woman quickly keyed in a series of codes then scanned her pass. Then she re-scanned the pizza and placed it in the baggage area.

There you are, lovely, she said. Have a good night and enjoy your pizza.

In the living room, the evening bled into night, and on TV the match was over, meaning the night was almost over too. The pundits in the studio were analysing Barcelona's high-pressing and he wondered where they'd all go after the match. He pictured the inside of the Irish bar off La Rambla, the one they went to for Peg's stag a few years back. Though the pundits were probably somewhere classier, a silver nightclub with an upstairs section cordoned off with a red rope. They'd be out there in Barcelona, late into the night, arguing about football over shots, meeting loads of new people, having a mad one, and he'd be in his bed in Abertridwr, because he had to be up early in the morning to go to a job he hated.

Do you know what's really shit about work? Big Mike said.

Everything, Peacock said. Peacock was lying on the opposite couch, not looking up from his phone.

Big Mike laughed. That's it, he said. It's just bullshit how it takes up my whole life, even when I'm not there.

I know mate, Peacock said. But it is what it is, isn't it?

I get paid fifteen grand a year, Big Mike said, and if I want to come home, turn on the football, and have a couple of beers, I can't really do that, can I? Because it would *affect* my *performance* at work.

Peacock looked up at him.

What the fuck you on about, Mikey? No one's stopping from you having a few cans.

Yeah, but I can't get wrecked, can I?

Free country, mate. Do what you like.

Yeah, but it's not though, is it? Not when you have to work.

Peacock's phone rang then, and he answered it all soft and cooing, like he was talking to a baby, and then he got up from the couch, nodded and smiled at Big Mike, and took the phone upstairs. Something about it didn't feel right. It was Big Mike's house, so the least Peacock could do was have the respect to stay around to watch till the end of the programme.

Peacock didn't respect him, though. If he did, he'd absolutely be offering to pay more rent, because it was a pisstake how little Peacock was paying now he had the new job. But if Big Mike asked him to pay more, and Peacock said no, what could he do? If Peacock moved out and left him on his own, he'd be completely fucked. The last couple of weeks Big Mike had been going over and over it when he couldn't sleep. Every time he opened the banking app, he found himself holding his breath. How on earth was this a life? He was thirty and he hadn't been near a woman in at least a year, and he could never afford a proper night out because the mortgage was crippling him. He knew he shouldn't think about it, because whenever he did, his chest would fill and then the fullness would rise to his neck and he'd feel like he was being strangled.

He could hear Peacock above him now, laughing in his room. He couldn't keep moaning to Peacock about work and shit, because if he whinged too much, it would only drive him away. He was just waiting for Peacock to come in one day and say he was leaving, or moving in with this Jess girl. They'd been on three dates, and she'd already stayed over once. Peacock hadn't even asked Big Mike's permission, he had just brought her back on a weeknight, and they'd been real loud in Peacock's room, laughing until, like, two in the morning. It had kept him up, but there was no point saying anything because he knew what Peacock was like. He'd be all sorry, and then just carry on doing exactly what he wanted to do.

He looked again at the photo from earlier: the stupid face, the swollen eyes. Why had he even taken the photo? He knew when he took it that he wasn't going to send it to anyone. On the way home, when he got stuck in traffic on St Martin's Road, he had looked at the photo again, and that's when he had the thought of digging up a fresh grave, drinking a bottle of drain cleaner, and just rolling himself in. He wouldn't be no harm to anyone then, and no one would have to deal with his body.

On the TV, the pundits were roundly praising Lionel Messi. Fair play, Messi was quality, but it was still odd that Barcelona had paid for Messi to have growth hormone treatment when he was a teenager. Because when you think about it, shouldn't growth hormones be classified as a performance-enhancing drug? When he was little, Big Mike had been a class footballer. Everyone said it. This one scout from Swansea City – Cliff Jones his name was – used to ring the house phone every Sunday night, and his mum would answer then put Mike on the line, and Cliff would tell Mike what a great game he had played earlier in the day, and how he was such a special talent. He went for trials down Swansea when he was twelve, and he played a few games for them and he did well, but in the end the coaches said he was just too small. It was such a shame, Cliff said, because Mikey honestly had the best technique he'd ever seen in a kid his age. We'll keep monitoring you, Cliff added, and if you do have a growth spurt – if you shoot up in your teens – we'll absolutely get you back down here with us, because you really are a little wizard.

He hadn't played in years now, though, because what was the point?

He looked at his tinder bio again. He wondered if he should delete the bit about being a short-arse. But what was he meant to do? At some point, the conversation about height was inevitably going to come up, or he would feel like he should mention it, and it wasn't like he could just lie, because if he ever did meet anyone, they would quickly see the truth. It was disgraceful, the amount of girls who wouldn't even look at a guy shorter than them. And worse than that, the real let-downs were the short girls – the five-foot-nothings – who wouldn't date him either, even though he had three inches on them. He once got into an argument about it with someone in a club.

I just like to feel protected, the woman said.

From what?

Crazy guys, she said. Crazy guys like you.

And he was a good-looking guy – that's what was so unfair. Sitting at his favourite spot in The Kings, the girls coming in were always giving him the eye, but then later, when he was standing at the bar waiting to be served he could feel those same girls giving him the twice-over: looking up and down, and then up and down again, just to make sure their eyes weren't fucked and that yes, he really was a fucking short-arse.

You're handsome, his best mate Rhian from school was always telling him. You've got a lovely face.

Well, marry me then, he wanted to say, and sometimes he did say that, and they'd both laugh, like *Imagine!*, and then they would both smile and that would be it, and then a little later Rhian would be talking about some shithead who'd been messing her around, not texting back, or who'd just been spotted in Cardiff getting off with another girl, and Big Mike would be raging inside, thinking: just give me a chance, why don't you?

She wouldn't, though, he knew that. It was out of the question. People were shallow. He could change himself, but there was just no changing people, so whatever he did didn't matter. He had tried Cuban heels, skinny jeans, and he grew a beard once. This was after he'd read an article where women were shown photos of men with and without beards and asked which they'd prefer to marry, and the women had overwhelmingly chosen the guys with beards.

The first few weeks his efforts were patchy and he was embarrassed every time he left the house. Peacock wound him up about it ('I think you've got something on your chin, mate!') – but that was just Peacock being Peacock, he was always taking the piss. After six weeks, though, Big Mike had a good, even spread, and in his bathroom mirror he thought he looked quite handsome. No one except Rhian had ever called him handsome before. He was feeling good about himself and then he went out with the boys to Cardiff, and when they were queuing to get into a club, an English stag party dressed like Where's Wally walked past, and one of the stag group grabbed him and went, 'Gnome!' and then another one came up to Big Mike and was like, 'Look at his little beard!' – and that was it, the Wallys went on their merry way. He was waiting for the boys to kick off, to go and chase the stag group halfway down the street, but the boys – his own pals – thought it was the funniest thing they'd ever heard, and for the rest of the night they kept stroking his chin and saying, 'Look at his little beard!'

The facial hair had taken six weeks to grow, and only minutes – at 3 a.m. that night – to drunkenly scrape off with a razor.

They should make everyone date in the dark, he thought. He'd seen the TV programme where they do that, and he just knew he'd absolutely thrive in that environment. Turn off the lights, and boom: he'd clear up, all the girls would be after him. But then, the lights would come on, and the girls would be like: *Aww, you're so cute, sorry though I'm gonna go with that smarmy dickhead over there, because he's five-foot-ten. Have a good life!*

The pundits on the telly were doing his head in now and the living room felt empty without Peacock. So he turned off the TV, and trudged up the stairs. A sheet of wallpaper was curling up at the ends, he could see the pink plaster underneath, and he couldn't believe it, because he'd only put the paper down like a year ago. He idled outside Peacock's room for a moment, thought about knocking, but he could hear him on the phone still, so he went to his own room and lay on the bed. Scrolling through messages, he had the same horrible sensation again: his hands weren't his own. He put his phone down and looked at them, the mad veins branching upwards towards his fingers. His hands felt cold, disowned. He was definitely going mad.

He called Rhian and very quickly found himself trying to explain what had been happening at work.

She just makes me feel thick as shit, he said. She's got me always second-guessing myself.

That's not good, Rhian said.

No, he said. And I dunno if I should file a complaint against her, cos she'd probably only worm her way out of it.

Yeah, Rhian said.

What do you think I should do?

I dunno Mikey, she said. But this has been going on a while, hasn't it? Don't get me wrong now, cos she doesn't sound great, but I just dunno if you're—

If I'm what?

No offence, she said, and don't be annoyed now, but do you know what your problem might actually be?

That I'm actually thick as shit?

Don't say that, she said.

I am though, aren't I?

You're not thick, she said.

I've got four GCSEs.

That doesn't mean anything.

Well, let's agree to disagree, he said. Anyway, tell me: what's my problem then?

He looked at his left hand; it really wasn't his.

You sure you really wanna hear this? she said.

Yeah, go on, he said. I can take it.

Well, to be honest, Mikey, I think you just don't really respect women.

What?

Like, in your job, I mean. I honestly don't think you can handle a woman telling you what to do.

Like hell, he said. Michelle is just a bitch, that's all.

Don't call her that, Rhian said.

Why not? She is one. She's a female dog.

It's sexist, Rhian said. And you can't go calling every woman you disagree with a bitch.

You call your mam a bitch, he said.

Rhian laughed. Well, that's different, she said.

How is that different?

Cos she actually *is* a bitch.

They both laughed then.

Oh look, he said. How about you save me the lecture for another night? I don't have the energy for an argument.

It's not an argument, she said. It's just some friendly advice from someone who knows you – and wants the best for you.

Yeah but—

Wait a minute, she said and then he could hear her shouting to someone.

Mam's calling me from downstairs, she said. Can I call you back?

He moped around his room for a bit then. It wasn't fair what Rhian was saying. He did respect women. Not liking his boss was nothing to do with her being a woman. From day one, when she swept into the place with all her hair, Michelle had acted like just because she'd been to university and had a business degree she knew everything there was to know about industrial waste disposal. She

made it seem like Big Mike's seven years in the job count-
ed for nothing. So while it was true that he didn't respect
Michelle as a boss, and that he did think she was a bitch,
none of that had anything to do with her being a woman.
Some people were just bitches. Though, thinking about it,
if she was a guy, he'd be calling her a dick instead, so there
was a difference, but it was nothing to do with respect.
It was just a different term, like the way you use 'actor'
for a guy, and 'actress' for a woman. There was nothing
disrespectful about it. The more he thought about it, he
really couldn't see where Rhian was coming from. It was
like the footballers' rape trial. All he had written on Facebook was that there was something *very strange* about
the case, and that the last time he checked, in this country you were innocent until proven guilty. But Rhian had
absolutely bitten his head off in the comments, saying he
didn't have a clue what he was on about and he should
just shut up. They properly fell out about that. In the end,
he apologised, and she was like, Wait, do you even know
why you're saying sorry? And he said, Yeah, cos I offended you. And that set her off all over again, and she was
like, Mikey, you're my friend, I love you, but you've got to
fucking wake up and see that the world is very different
for you than it is for me. He couldn't get on board with
that, though, because the world was just the world, wasn't
it? It was shit for everyone, and anyway, he couldn't see
what any of this had to do with the law. Rhian totally lost
it then. She told him to *grow up,* to *cop the fuck on,* and
to *really think* about what he was saying, because he had

no idea what it was like being a woman. She told him not to get back in touch until he finally learned some empathy. It took weeks until they properly made up.

She called back now.

Sorry about that, she said. Where were we?

You were saying I'm sexy?

She laughed.

Nice try, she said. Sex*ist*. Mind you, I've always said you're a good-looking boy.

He smiled at that, glad they were back on good terms.

Up to anything this weekend then? he asked.

Ah, I dunno, she said. I'm skint.

Me too, he said. All I've got is eighteen quid to last me till pay day on Monday.

We make a right pair, don't we? she said.

When she said things like that, his heart would judder.

Wanna do something Saturday then? he said. Something that doesn't cost any money. You could come over and we could have some food and watch a film if you fancy it?

Yeah, that could be good. Let me see how the rest of the week goes, though. It's been quite busy already this week so by the time the weekend comes I might just wanna flop.

Cool, he said. Well I'll give you a text on Friday anyway.

Lovely, she said, and there was a pause, and then she said, Be honest Mikey, are you still pissed off with me about what I said earlier? I know what you're like with stuff like this. If I don't ask, you'll never say.

He laughed. Well, I'm a little bit pissed off, he said. But I'm still inviting you over, so it can't be too bad, can it?

I just don't like it when you're down, she said. And if you're really not happy, you should do something about it.

Like what though? he said, and he knew he sounded defensive.

I dunno. Look for another job? Do something different?

I can't quit my job, he said. I've got the car to pay out on. And a mortgage.

I'm not saying quit your job, am I? I'm saying just have a think about what else you could do. Or what you'd like to do.

But what if I get a new job and hate it as much as this one?

Then you find another job. We've gotta take some risks, or otherwise we'd never leave the house.

Says the girl who's been in the same job for ten years.

Eight years, she said. And I happen to like my job! That's the difference.

He laughed.

Fair point, he said.

I'm gonna go to bed now, she said. I've had terrible sleep all week.

Alright then, he said. Well good luck sleeping tonight.

Thank you, she said. You too. Nos da.

Nos da, he said.

After they hung up, he opened his folder of Rhian photos on his phone. He had a lot of photos of her. Cupping his mouth with his hands, he let out a long, long sigh.

He opened tinder again and began to swipe. The problem with a lot of the girls around here was that they were absolutely obsessed with CrossFit. Half their photos were them in a mirror with a six-pack. He couldn't be with anyone like that, they'd laugh him out of the bedroom with the little gut he had going on. He swiped through faces, his heart twinging every time a positive swipe wasn't instantly returned. After fifteen minutes, tinder told him there was no one else left in the area, so he expanded the range from twenty miles to thirty miles and found a lovely girl in Brecon. Her name was Hannah. She was twenty-seven and she had such a nice face. In one picture, she was at a Wales game and she was wearing a Wales shirt, so that was a good sign. There wouldn't be any hassle getting to watch the matches. He scrolled down to read her profile. At the bottom, beside an asterisk, she had written: *5'10 – not looking for anyone shorter, sorry guys!!*

Seriously.

Shit like this drove him mad.

He googled 'short people discrimination' and read a piece about unconscious bias. Being a short man in the workplace was basically worse than being a woman. If he was five-four, he'd be getting another 800 quid a year now. Five-five, and we're talking an extra 1,600 quid per annum. It wasn't that people were doing it intentionally, well, not everyone, but he just knew that people didn't take him seriously because of his height. What could he do, though? It wasn't like he could form a union, the Short-Arse Protest Society, to march through Cardiff.

Everyone would laugh at them. And that's the thing, short people were always the punchline. Except with Rhian. She was always really good about it, and she never teased or took the piss.

He got up from bed. He could see the light was still on in Peacock's room. But when he crossed the landing, he heard a click and the light under his door disappeared.

He went back to his own room. He looked at Rhian's Facebook page now. He went through all her profile photos, all the way back to the first one from when she first got the account. She really was a pretty girl. And she was sound, too. That's what was good about hanging out with her, they just got on, things were never a hassle.

He WhatsApped her: you still up?

One tick.

Two ticks.

Then came the dot-dot-dot which indicated she was writing. And then it disappeared.

He sighed and got up. From his underwear drawer he took out the lovely thick dark green socks his nan got him for his birthday. Sat on the edge of his bed, his ankle over his knee, he peeled off the thin grey pair he'd worn to work, and tossed them, balled up, into the laundry bag. Putting the thick socks on, his feet felt hugged and everything seemed a little bit better. He padded downstairs, the steps softer now, and moved into the kitchen. He took his favourite Manchester United mug from the cupboard and made himself a tea with two sugars, helping himself to a couple of Cadbury's chocolate fingers.

He looked at his phone: Rhian wasn't online, and he wondered if she had fallen asleep. She did that sometimes, she'd just nod off with the phone in her hand. They'd be chatting away, and then her voice would get softer and softer, and then she'd just be out like a light. Ah, she was great though. And the best thing was they were already friends, they'd been friends since school, so they already knew everything and didn't have to explain themselves to each other. She had known his mam and the two of them had properly loved each other. When she was fourteen, Rhian had basically moved in. This was after she'd stopped talking to her own mother cos she'd been force-feeding her. She just started coming round after school and having dinner with them, and his own mam wouldn't say a word about Rhian only eating tiny portions. She knew the whole story, of how Rhian had got it into her head that her mother was trying to poison her and how she'd pinned Rhian down on the kitchen floor, trying to force a potato into her mouth. He could see why Rhian's mam did that – it had been getting stupid how little she'd been eating – but you don't go force-feeding your daughter on the kitchen floor. That stuff was madness.

He sat at the kitchen table and drank his tea now, dipping the chocolate fingers until the chocolate was melty. Outside, it was wet and dark, the rain pebble-dashing against the window. That's what was so shit about having a job: in the morning you go to work and it's dark, and then you come home and it's dark. The only bit of natural light he got was in his lunch hour, when he'd go over to Caerphilly Castle with a bag of oats to feed the ducks. Standing on the banking, as the waddling ducks gathered and flapped around him, he'd lift his face to the heavens, as if to better absorb the vitamin D from the dark grey sky. He wasn't as bad as Rhian with it, though. She had full on SAD. She had to get up an hour early just to sit in front of a lamp – otherwise she'd just stay in bed all day, for days on end.

He googled 'labradors' then. He had always loved the idea of having a chocolate Labrador. If he ever got one, he'd name it Arnold and he would take it for walks up Caerphilly Mountain. Rhian could come, too, she could bring her mam's dog, Perry. They could let them both off the lead to run about the place and smell each other's bums. Afterwards, he and Rhian could get burgers from the Mountain Snack Bar, sit down on the picnic benches, and he'd let Arnold have a bite. Maybe he'd get Arnold a burger all for himself. It could be a thing they'd do every Sunday. *My favourite customers,* the guy at the shack would say. *Perry and Arnold!*

Maybe he could actually set up a dog-walking business. He would be able to spend all day outside then, he could free the locked-up dogs who spend all day inside, and take them to parks and hills, running through wet grass, the air fresh on his face. There were so many beautiful places around the Valleys that no one knew about. Yeah, maybe he'd buy himself a 4x4 or a big van and load it up with dogs, and spend the day hanging out with mutts, having a laugh. That would be the life. Him and Rhian could do a bit of dog-grooming on the side. *Wanna Mohawk, mate?*

God, Rhian really was the best though. And she didn't know it, either. He liked that about her. She wasn't stuck up. He looked at her Instagram now, scrolled through to the selfie they took together a few months ago at Party in the Park. Fair play, she looked lush in that photo and there wasn't even a filter on it. She was naturally gorgeous, she just was.

His phone vibrated.

Finally, a reply from Rhian: Yeah can't sleep. what's up?

Without a further thought, he typed: Do u really think i dont respect women?? – and then he looked at the text, and held his finger on the backspace until it was all deleted, all blank. He paused a moment, biting his thumb, and then he wrote: I dont wanna mess things up between us and you can tell me to piss off if you like but if i dont ask you now i don't think i ever will. So Im taking a risk for once in my life. Do you wanna go on a date?

One tick.

Two ticks.

She had read the message, but there was nothing, no reply.

He waited a few minutes, his body flooding with fear as his strange hands cupped his flushing face, and when he could bear it no longer, he sent a follow-up: ???

One tick.

Two ticks.

The shimmering ellipsis . . .

                  and then his screen

    filled . . .

        up . . .

              with . . .

        words.

Passenger

Up on the hill together, they look down at the glittering sea. It's beautiful – or at least that's what he's probably supposed to think – but Geraint doesn't know what he's meant to do with the view. Just look? He takes a photo, sends it to his mum.

36 degrees! he writes.

Ice lolly? Niamh says, eyeing the ice-cream van.

Inspired idea, says Geraint.

In the final steps towards the van, Geraint subtly slows his tread so that Niamh will arrive ahead of him and she can do the talking.

Okay? the man at the van says.

Very okay, Niamh says, then turning to Geraint: What are you having?

I think I'll . . . yeah . . . I'll have the chocolate thing, he says. The Lino Lado.

That's boring, she says. I wanted that one too.

I can have something else, he says. I don't mind.

You will not, she says.

He hands Niamh a hundred-kuna note, but she bats it away.

Settled on a nearby wall with their ice-creams, they look out over the view again.

This is alright, isn't it? she says.

Not bad at all, he says.

A black cat emerges from a bush, then stretches out beside them in the shade.

Well hello handsome, Niamh says, reaching down to stroke its chin. Looking for an ice-choc sandwich, are you?

I wouldn't be sure he speaks English, Geraint says.

Ah, he definitely understands me. Don't you mister? Oh, look at your little tuxedo! You must very be very hot.

While Niamh is on her hunkers petting the cat, Geraint spots the bus driver standing at the edge of the road. The driver is heavy-looking, the top button of his white collared shirt undone, his chest hair curling out. He is texting and frowning. Geraint wonders what any of this means to the driver, how regularly he makes this drive up the hill then back down again. Something in the driver's stance reminds Geraint of his father.

Do you think there's room in the suitcase for this little fella? Niamh says, rubbing the cat's tummy.

It'll be a tight squeeze, but I think we can do it.

Excellent, she says. How's your Lino Lado?

Ten out of ten, he says.

You've surprised me there, she says. Because I'd have given it more of an eight.

Back on the bus, the bus driver glugs water from a litre bottle. He rubs his face, then flings his phone onto the dash. He seems pissed off about something. Geraint remembers an argument he once had with his dad after his father told him that the whole two-litres-a-day thing was just a marketing ploy devised by Evian. He was never quite sure when his father was being serious, and when he was just looking for a reaction.

COME ON! the driver yells to the remaining passengers, who are still outside taking photos. Geraint grimaces, and the other passengers amble back on onboard, as the driver tuts and shakes his head.

When the automatic door closes shut, the driver rolls his shoulders and turns around.

BELTS! he shouts. BELTS ON!

And everything – the jabbing lurching of the engine as the driver turns the key, the way he roughly steers and jerks around corners – everything seems pissed off and resentful. Geraint pictures the bus driver jabbing a finger in his face, screaming abuse.

You foreigners are so fucking incapable. You can't even drive.

But is the atmosphere as tense as this, really? Because looking at Niamh and the other passengers, they don't seem all that bothered.

When they hit traffic, the driver lights a cigarette. Geraint watches and breathes deep. The air is dry and his throat constricts, as panic slowly fills his gut. A dormant neural pathway illumines and his shoulders scrunch. He is eight years old, sitting up front in his father's car, beside an ashtray of stubby cigarettes. There's always a sense of threat on these summer visits with his father. He's never quite sure what this man will do. Today they're going on a drive and he doesn't know where. He imagines his father suddenly veering off the road and accelerating straight into a wall. They are pulling up at a pavement on an unfamiliar road in an unfamiliar town now, and his father tells Geraint he'll be back in ten minutes. The thud of the closing door marks the beginning of a new passage of time and place; the car is a sealed box with only Geraint inside. Through the windscreen, he watches his father stand mutely on the pavement. His father is looking around, and then he walks away. Without him, another scene is happening elsewhere: his father is meeting someone, buying something, having conversations with strangers. And Geraint is alone in his father's car – the seatbelt pressing tight across his chest, his restless shoes tapping in the footwell.

His phone vibrates.

Looks.lovely, his mother replies. *Hope ur having a good time and don't burn. The boiler man can't come until Tuesday so I've still got no hot water.*

Back in Old Town, they walk around, looking at things, not knowing what to do. Approaching a church, they stand in the doorway but do not enter. Are they allowed to go in? At independent stores in Dublin, Geraint becomes anxious if he sees a staircase. Is he allowed upstairs? Will someone shout at him? He can tell that Niamh wants to cross the threshold, but with his hands on his hips he leans back and angles his shoulders away from the door. His feet are facing the church, but he is looking in another direction. Why did he think he would – or could – behave any differently abroad?

So here they come again, back to the water fountain at the centre of the square.

It's *very* hot, Niamh says.

So hot, Geraint agrees.

Evening comes as a relief.

Leaving the hotel, the temperature is 30 degrees; and though his blood is still gurgling warm in his veins, the air feels bearable at least.

What do you fancy eating?

I don't mind, what are you thinking?

For twenty-five minutes they traipse round alleys and squares, nervously approaching menus and avoiding eye-contact with over-eager waiters. They finally settle for noodles at a Thai restaurant, where the food is perfectly fine, though the staff seem sad.

When they're almost done with their food, Niamh's phone vibrates.

It's mam, she says, sighing.

You can answer, Geraint says, finishing off his wine.

I don't want to, Niamh says, resting her phone face downwards on the table. I can't be dealing with her. She's on such a high right now.

Geraint lays a hand on her shoulder, and Niamh stares off, lost to him.

And then the manager comes to take away their plates.

Good? she asks.

Lovely, Geraint says, thank you so much.

The table cleared, Niamh exhales.

Well, she says.

Cocktails, Geraint replies. Sangria, pints of vodka, let's drink them all.

At a bar across the way, an attractive barman brings out complimentary shots. Geraint doesn't want shots, but it seems like a challenge – an entryway into the kingdom of actual fun.

Go on then, he says, and Geraint and Niamh and the barman knock back a shot of something bitter and sweet.

Tonight will be a good night! the barman says, and he laughs and wipes his lips.

After two glasses of beer, Niamh says to Geraint, So what's up?

Nothing's up.

Something's not right, she says. I've thought it all day. You seem off.

I'm fine, he says. It's probably just the heat. Are you alright?

It's like you're not here, she says.

What do you mean?

I mean, you're miles away a lot of the time, but I dunno, it's like you haven't even arrived yet. You're somewhere else.

Where am I then?

I don't know, that's why I'm asking.

Well, I'm here, he says, patting himself. I'm a hundred per cent here.

Okay, she says. Fair enough. I think I need to stretch my legs. Will we go for a walk?

They walk along the dock, past a succession of glamorous women posing against railings – their muscular partners standing back to take their photos. For fun, Niamh gets Geraint to pose against the railings and he obliges, happy to be able to do something silly.

Work it baby, she says, directing him to look over his shoulder. More flirty! Give your fans what they want.

He laughs, and Niamh takes his picture, then immediately looks at it on her phone.

I don't want to see it, Geraint says.

Aw, you look so pretty.

If it goes online, I'm suing.

I'll see you in court, she says.

Down by the sea they settle down on some rocks. A guy approaches with a carrier bag of beers, and they buy two cans and look out at people partying on boats.

I'm going to turn my phone off before Mam calls again, Niamh says. Does that make me an awful person?

Absolutely, Geraint replies. A dreadful, awful person.

It just makes me feel so knotty, she says. I love her, but she's legit batshit right now.

I'm sorry.

It's really not fair, she says. Like, Dad's the one who left her in the lurch for thirty years, and now she's the one who's ended up thinking she can talk to the dead.

Geraint laughs.

Any further updates on that one? he says.

I swear to god, Niamh says. I bet that's why she was calling earlier. She wanted to tell me all about her recent sightings. Either that, or she was only calling to give out again about abortions. '*It's Satanic! I told you we shouldn't have signed the Lisbon Treaty!*'

Yeah, that's a bit intense alright, Geraint says. I'm sorry you have to deal with all that.

It's just shit how it worked out, Niamh says. Because Dad was always working abroad, Mam's the one had to do all the hard work, you know? She did most of the discipline, all the cooking, all the cleaning, while he just got to be the *fun* dad coming back with cool presents. I used to feel guilty when I was little because I preferred spending time with him. He was just more relaxed. And I probably still prefer spending time with him now, even though I know that his *shite* is half the reason Mam is like she is. And now he's retired, he's back living in the house full time, but they barely talk. He just parks himself in the office upstairs, sending emails to us all.

Geraint shakes his head. Sounds like perfectly normal behaviour, he says, and Niamh laughs at the absurdity of it all.

But seriously, Geraint says, that is a lot for you to deal with. How's your brother finding it now your dad's back in the house?

Niamh lets out a shallow sigh.

Actually, she says, do you mind if we don't talk about this any more? It's already taken up too much of the conversational pie chart.

Yeah, of course, Geraint says.

Thanks, she says.

And there's a pause, a long moment of silence, and then she says: What's the craic with you and your dad anyway? You still haven't explained the half of it.

Oh, I don't want to drag you into all that.

Do you feel like I'm dragging you into all my stuff?

No! That's not what I meant.

Then why wouldn't I want to hear about it?

It's not that I think you wouldn't want to hear. But I dunno, it would just be weird. I don't know where I'd start.

An older couple climb past, smile, offering a little wave.

Evening, Niamh says.

Good evening, the couple reply.

Look, you don't have to talk about any of it, Niamh says. It's just I'm always talking to you about my stuff. You're a good listener.

Thank you, he says.

You don't have to say thank you. It wasn't a compliment. It was a statement of fact!

Mum's always said I'm a good listener. She said I always have been since I was a kid. When her sisters used to come around to visit, I'd sit under the table and listen to them talk for hours.

That's cute, Niamh says. Well, either cute or you were just a big snoop. I wonder if we'd have liked each other when we were kids.

I reckon I'd have been intimidated.

Why?

Cos you were a really pretty girl! And your father had you wearing a Dolce & Gabbana belt.

Yeah, Niamh says, laughing. That didn't help my cause. Everyone in school thought I was so stuck up. A rich bitch.

Geraint pulls a performatively considered look.

Are you saying I was a rich bitch, Geraint Jones?

Well, in fairness, I don't know what little Niamh was like back then. I've only got the adult Niamh's reports to go on.

Count yourself lucky, she says, taking a sip of her can. At least she gives you reports. Based on what you've told me – and from what I've observed this last little while – all I know is that you were probably a smug, sporty child.

Geraint laughs.

Smug, he says.

I'm just going on what I've observed, she says.

Alright then, he says. What else do you want to know?

I want to know what you were like as a kid, she says. Or, I don't know . . . what was life like for you, in *Wales*?

She says Wales with a strong put-on Welsh accent.

I think we had very different childhoods, he says.

Obviously, she says. Like, it doesn't have to be anything deep or meaningful. But, I dunno, I just want to have a picture of what you were like, what growing up was like, all that craic.

Geraint sips his beer and gives another performed look of thoughtfulness.

Oh come on, she says. Tell me something funny from when you were little. You must have something.

Alright, he says, resting his can on a rock. He squints skywards and nods. Okay, this is a ridiculous story. When I was ten years old, I was saving up for this new pair of trainers. They were Adidas, green and black and white. I used to go visit them in the sports shop in town. I was in love with them. They were £16, I remember that. So I started saving away, putting all the money I made into my savings account.

What money were you making at ten years old?

Oh you know what I mean. Pocket money and birthday money and a quid here and there doing jobs for my aunts and stuff like that. Anyway, I was saving away, then one day my mother took me into the Abbey National and I withdrew all the money I had in my account – £14 – and the man at the counter was like, 'Ooh, what are you going to spend all that money on? Something nice?' And I was like, *Oh it's not for me, it's to pay our water rates.*

Geraint laughs.

My mum's face, he says. Oh god.

Your poor mam, Niamh says, softly. And poor you.

Oh no, he says. It's not like that. It was funny, really. And she paid me back in the end.

I don't think it is funny, she says. Imagine being your mam in that situation.

Ah, it was fine, he says.

But only now, twenty years later, does he pause to reconsider the scene.

Niamh is looking at him. He smiles weakly, but her eyes are sad, and he feels the story sinking in for them both. His heart is beating fast, and his throat is pulsing. The stillness, the silence, the look on Niamh's face, it's pulling him somewhere he doesn't want to go.

Pub? he finally says.

Yeah? she asks.

Aye, he says. Let's find a pub.

So they head on and end up at a bar, where they fall into conversation with an Austrian man named Stephen who keeps asking Geraint about the Manic Street Preachers.

Does he love them? (Geraint says he likes some of their songs, but wouldn't say he's a huge fan.)

Has he ever met any of the band? (No, he hasn't.)

What it's like, the town where the Manics are from? (Blackwood is fine, he says, and the new cinema is lovely!)

What do you think happened to Richey Edwards? (No idea.)

So how long have you two been *an item*? Stephen asks.

Almost nine months? Geraint says.

Yeah, something like that, Niamh says. Depends how you define it I suppose, but yeah, around that.

You're almost ready to be born then! Stephen says.

Yeah, we're just fetuses, Niamh replies.

That is good, Stephen says. But as James Dean Bradfield says: *If you tolerate this then your children will be next.*

The joke doesn't make sense, but Geraint humours Stephen with a laugh. Is it his job to get rid of Stephen, or to suggest to Niamh they go someplace else? It jitters inside, not knowing if it's his place to make the call. So he leaves for a pee, though what he actually wants is some time out.

Sitting on the toilet, looking at his phone, he realises he's pretty drunk. His mother's message is still there, still un-replied to:

Looks.lovely. Hope ur having a good time and don't burn. The boiler man can't come until Tuesday so I've still got no hot water.

He starts writing a reply then realises he doesn't know what to say. He really is very drunk, the ceiling is moving, it won't stay still. When he was little, they never went on holidays, but in summer he and his mother would wait for the grant to come in – the £100 school-uniform grant – and then they'd go to the nearest big town and buy his new uniform and then go to the big sports shop to buy trainers for his sports kit. That was the best part, picking out the trainers. If they had some money left over at the end, his mother would buy them an ice cream each, which he always felt guilty about because he was worried some-one from the school or government would find out. He sits on the toilet now, and reads his mother's message again:

Looks.lovely. Hope ur having a good time and don't burn. The boiler man can't come until Tuesday so I've still got no hot water.

He stares at the cubicle door, thinking of the yellowed kitchen cupboard where his mother would leave pocket money for him, his brother, and his sister. A small stack of coins each week. A pound maybe? A pound-fifty on a good week, 75p on a bad one, or maybe just 50p, but always something, always some small thing to allow him some dignity and independence. She fought to give him this – give them all this – while the house was falling down, while there was damp in the walls and the wallpaper peeled away in curls and the joists were rotten, and there was mould in the bathroom and the wind whistled at night through the crack in his bedroom window, a thin breeze that made his cheeks cold. In the cubicle in Croatia, he is back there now, back standing alone in the living room, waiting for the inspector from the council to arrive, waiting weeks, months, years, waiting to discover if the council deems their family worthy enough of help.

All I'm saying is that you're not free if you can't drive, the Austrian man is saying now back at the bar.

Hey, Niamh says, wrapping her arm around Geraint's waist. Stephen wants to know why we can't drive.

Geraint laughs.

I've just never got round to learning, he says. Living in a city, there's just no need.

But you should learn to drive, man, Stephen says. Otherwise you're stuck.

I like walking, Geraint says, stifling a hiccup.

I think I do want to learn soon though, Niamh says.

Really? Geraint says.

Yeah. I don't think I'll feel like an adult until I do.

Oh, Geraint says. You've never said that before.

Dude, Stephen says. Learn to drive, man. And then you can take this woman real places.

This woman? Niamh says, laughing.

Oh forgive me, Stephen says. I didn't realise I was talking to a feminist.

Geraint puts his hands on Niamh's arm. Drink? he says.

She looks at him.

Nah, I think I've reached my limit, Niamh says. I think you might have too?

My apologies if I have offended you, Stephen says.

Nah, you're fine, Niamh says. We've just had a long one.

Geraint rubs his eyes, yawns.

Niamh's hand is resting on the inside of his thigh.

Come on, she says. Leaba time.

Beneath a glowing moon, they walk back to the hotel arm in arm, delighted at how drunk they are.

This *woman!* Geraint declares to the sky, laughing.

Back in their room, Niamh unbuttons Geraint's shirt, strokes his chest and pushes him onto the bed. He slips inside her and he can feel the sweat on her ass while she rides him. She bites her lip now, and he lifts his finger to her lips and she sucks it. You're so fucking hot, he says, his hands on her breasts, and he looks up at her perfect smiling mouth and he suddenly believes that he is genetically inferior to Niamh. He should never have told her about the stuff with his mum and the money. Now that she can see him as he was, as he really is, she will one day leave him for someone with whom her offspring will be thriving, pulsing humans; someone not pitted and pocked and sad, someone whose genetics are not corrupted by a lifetime of being poor.

I love you, he says, as they lie beside each other.

Mm, she says, her voice gently drifting off. Me too. This woman is sleepy.

*

Sitting on the steps of a public building in Old Town, Dubrovnik, he watches other tourists walking by, wondering how everyone else seems so at ease.

Pizza? Geraint says.

I don't think I could do any more pizza, Niamh says.

What about that place?

Niamh takes a sip of her water. Nah, I don't trust the font.

If you could eat anything in the world, what would it be?

Why is it always what I want?

Cos I'm easy, he says. I'll eat anything.

And so the day passes.

*

Sitting on the steps of a museum in Old Town, Dubrovnik, he watches other tourists walking by, wondering how everyone else is so comfortable in their skin.

What should we do then? Niamh says.

I don't mind, Geraint says. I'm easy.

He wipes his forehead.

It's just so hot, he says.

Thirty-seven degrees, she says.

Should we get some lunch?

Good idea, she says. What do you fancy?

I don't mind, he says. I'm easy. I could eat whatever.

You keep saying that, she says, but seriously, you're not.

And so the day passes.

*

Sitting on the steps down to the beach in Hvar, he watches other tourists walking by. This is his life now, watching other people live.

I need a pee, Niamh says.

My feet are tired, he says.

Do we have any water left?

I'm a little bit hungry.

I've got a bit of a headache.

My eye is twitching.

I think I got bitten.

I'm just a bit tired.

Should we go back to the hotel for a little lie-down?

You'll feel better after a nap.

It's just so hot though.

Do you have any water left?

And so the day passes.

*

Sitting on the steps down to the quay in Split, he regards themselves as characters in *Sims* – with status bars for hunger and bladder and sleep and hygiene and energy and fun; if these bars ever elapse, it's game over.

Though lying in bed now, Niamh asleep beside him, the fan whirring, his body exhausted, he is moved by their patience and concern for one another's biology.

He still can't sleep, though, his mind is lapping. He is among the squares and the alleys, walking around in loops, Niamh's bobbing head always in the frame, as they try to get to the thing, whatever the thing even is. He re-reads old emails from her on his phone now. A few months back, she sent him a very long email, ending:

I don't get why you're so nervous around me all the time. Am I that intimidating? When I ask you to put on some music I can see you agonising, like you're afraid you're going to get it wrong. I think you're brilliant and I think you're kind and thoughtful but for some reason you're holding back and it's causing me to wonder if it's something I'm doing, if I'm somehow responsible for holding you back? Please tell me if it is and I'll try and be different. But right now it's really hard for me to be fully myself when I don't think you're being yourself.

I want to open up to you, I really do, but I don't know how to do it if you won't let me in. I want us to be ourselves with each other but I don't know how we start if you're not showing up?? Sometimes I hear you on the phone to your friends and you are laughing so much and I can hear you sounding so confident and normal and spontaneous. I know that there's another you that i rarely see. I know he's in there somewhere so why don't I see him?

He reads the last paragraph over and over.

*

When he wakes, Niamh is already up and dressed.

I'm going to go out for a bit, she says.

Well, wait up and I'll come too.

Nah, she says. Stay here, have a read or something.

No, he says. It's fine. Just give me five minutes.

I think I'd actually like to be on my own for a bit, she says.

Oh.

I think it'll be good for the both of us, she says, pulling a tote bag over her shoulder. Just, you know—

Yeah, he says. That makes sense. A bit of space and—

Yeah, she says. Let's text and meet up for lunch.

Cool, he says. Very cool.

Without her, the room is quiet. Alone, it dawns on him that he had wanted this time to himself all along, but now that she has gone, there's a ditch in his stomach – deep and dark – and everything is collapsing into the hole.

She's gone, says a voice from the soil.

Geraint turns over and punches the bed.

In town on his own, he feels utterly lost. He has no idea what to do, where to go, how to make a plan. He just walks and walks and checks his phone constantly. Sitting down on the steps of a church he thinks: she has seen through me, has seen there's nothing there, just a hollow shell of a person, trying to reflect back whatever she wants or needs. When he's with her, he loses all sense of himself. Everything gets shrunk down to what she needs and how he can provide it.

His gut is churning. Inside the churning, he is turning over and over, punching beds, tables, walls.

A voice then, a whisper:

You're in a fucking pickle, aren't you?

At lunch, Niamh seems brighter, lighter, showing off a pair of earrings she's bought her mam.

She'll love these, she says, and Geraint finds it in himself to return a bright smile.

But his stomach is still churning.

Later, in a public bathroom he rushes to a cubicle and the first shit plunks out, followed by a dark wet gush, and more and more stringy wet shit. It smells awful. He wipes and wipes then gets shit on his hands. At the sink he scrubs and scrubs using multiple servings of soap, but hovering his hands under the too-hot hand-dryer, he knows he'll feel dirty until he can shower. When he emerges outside, wiping the last of the dampness into his shorts, he thinks there's something newly resigned in Niamh's nod. As she moves away from the wall, giving him back his bag, he detects a certain head-loneliness, as if she's returning from sullen thoughts. She is sick of him, he is sure. Their relationship is failing a test; the cliff is crumbling, their house teetering on the edge.

In the shower that evening he scrubs and scrubs until he feels wholly clean and worthy of her body.

They go for dinner and have strained chat over a bottle of wine, and when Geraint suggests heading to a bar, Niamh says, Actually, can we go back to the hotel?

In their room, he boils the kettle and makes them each a peppermint tea. When he hands it to her, she says thank you very softly. He climbs onto the bed, then places his cup on the side table. Niamh rests her cup down on the carpet and drops her head into his lap.

I can't do this for another fifty years, she says.

He strokes her hair. What's *this*? he says

I don't know. My life? I don't know what my life even is. Like, my job is just so unimportant. If I didn't turn up, nothing would change.

I get that.

And my family's nuts, she says, and they're only going to get weirder as they get older. And I keep writing these stupid little things that don't amount to anything. I'm just wasting my time.

I've told you I'd love to read what you're writing.

When I was back home I could just keep going, you know? But now I've stopped for a minute, it's – I dunno.

119

She's throbbing, he can feel it off her. He strokes her head now, feels the shape of her skull. Closing his eyes, he pictures the darkness of space and pinpricks of light. They're passing through her mind and body, all these galaxies of feeling. But he feels partially relieved it's her life that's bothering her, and not him.

Niamh shifts from his lap, and sits up now.

How can I help? he says.

It's not for you to solve, she says. It's just *everything*. What the fuck am I doing? I'm thirty. I'm not young.

You're not old either, he says. You've got plenty of time. You can change what you're doing.

Yeah but – I dunno. You say I've got plenty of time, and maybe I do, but I also feel like I don't have many moves left. I can't fuck up whatever I do next.

I know what you're saying, he says.

And then they're both silent, as she takes deep sighs and he strokes her leg.

As if he can't resist pushing, he finally asks: Are we alright?

That's not what this is about, she says.

I know that—

It's not us, she says.

Yeah, I know, but I'm asking anyway.

Well, we're stuck, aren't we? she says. There's this wall between us, isn't there? I thought we'd have broken through by now.

Okay, he says.

Sometimes when we're fucking, I think we're going to

120

break through. It feels so close, but then we just go back to being us again.

I feel that too, he says.

He goes to kiss her, but it's as if everything is too heavy and she sort of collapses in his arms.

We're okay, he says, holding her tight.

Later, when she's asleep, he googles cafes and restaurants and museums. To access the museum site, he has to join the mailing list. He provides an old hotmail address, an account he mostly uses for signing online petitions and accessing free Wi-Fi in public spaces. To proceed to the exhibition info, the museum website asks him to confirm the Sign Up. He hasn't logged into the account in months; the inbox is full of unread promotional emails. After he confirms the museum email, he finds himself typing his father's name into the search bar. He reads again the last message his father sent him. In its entirety, the message says:

> I have got used to having no contact from you so this development is hardly going to have any further impact on my life.

*

I'm sorry for my *display* last night, Niamh says next morning.

Don't be, he says.

I put a lot on you.

121

You don't, he says.

I know I do, she says. I need to go back to therapy. Once I get some money. But let's not lose another day talking about all this. What will we do today anyway?

We can talk about it anytime, he says.

Please, she says.

Alright, he says. Well, I actually found this really good-looking sandwich place last night. They've got these mad elaborate sandwiches that look great. And then I found this cool-looking rock bar. God knows what 'rock' actually means in Croatia? But it's got a couple of good reviews. Does that sound like a plan?

She smiles. Is this you being assertive?

It is indeed.

Look at you! she says. I'm proud.

And as they get ready for the day, he feels like something has shifted, as if he has steadied the scales, as if he might even be in charge.

But after the sandwiches turn out to be just alright, and they're climbing the stairs to the rock bar, he feels a sinking worry in his blood. He imagines the metal-head bar-staff cross-examining and eviscerating his taste in music. ('The Strokes? That isn't rock! Get the fuck out of here.') But when he and Niamh enter, the actual bar is empty, except for one other patron: an older woman, in the corner, drinking a glass of beer. She is wearing a black boater hat.

What are you having? Geraint says to Niamh.

I'm still crammed from that massive Ćevapi, she says. Can you get me something light? I'll be back now. I'm just gonna go find the toilets.

There are no taps at the bar, just a tall fridge beside the jukebox. Sensing the gaze of the boater woman, he looks up. She tips her hat, and gestures for him to open the fridge. It seems presumptuous, but the woman is watching, and he pictures Niamh returning from the toilet to find him standing there like a child seeking adult permission to enter a friend's house. He takes two lagers off the shelf, and as he turns around, a man roars, NO! What are you doing?

BACK IN THE FRIDGE! the man shouts, and Geraint returns the drinks.

What beer you want? the man says.

Geraint stammers his answer and the barman sighs and takes the exact same bottles from the fridge. Behind the bar he roughly levers off the caps, plonking the beers down on the counter.

Never take beers from the fridge, he says. It's not your bar.

Opening his wallet, Geraint's hands are shaking. He leaves a large tip on the counter, something inside of him shrivelling.

He takes the beers to a table as far from the bar as possible. Waiting for Niamh, he doesn't know how to hold himself. He looks around, sipping his bottle, trying to project that he's unfazed, but his face is hot, his ears are burning.

Finally, Niamh returns smiling.

These looks good, she says, taking her beer.

I hope it's light enough for you, he says.

Iechyd da, she says, raising her bottle to his.

Sláinte, he replies, and they clink.

Niamh takes her first sip.

That's tasty, she says. You chose well.

When Niamh begins to take interest in the framed vinyl on the walls, he tries to smile, but his lips are wooden. The boater woman is looking over. He worries she'll come to their table and mention the incident, or that the barman will make some belittling or chummy joke about the fridge.

I could really do with some real art for my room, she says.

Mhhm, Geraint says

Though I still don't know what the landlord thinks about us drilling stuff.

Yeah, he says.

Did your landlady get back to you about the toilet?

I haven't said anything to her yet.

It's been leaking three months! she says.

I know, he says, but we don't want to bother her. I figure the less bother we are, the less chance she'll put up the rent.

Well, she can't just randomly put up the rent can she?

Yeah, I know, but – you know what I mean. Like, there's less chance she'll kick us out and get in new people.

She can't do that either!

Geraint looks at her.

Well, legally speaking, she says.

Yeah, he says. I should say something. Or maybe I'll do a plumbing course and fix the toilet myself.

Niamh laughs.

You know what, she says. I wouldn't put it past you to actually do a plumbing course just so that you could avoid any kind of conflict with your landlady.

Geraint opens his arms.

Fear of conflict, he says. Don't knock it till you've tried it.

Niamh sighs, then laughs.

When she's finished her beer, Geraint says, Let's go somewhere else.

Really? she says

Over at the fridge the barman is rearranging the bottles.

Yeah, he says. Let's keep racking up the memories.

Okay, she says.

As they leave, Niamh says thank you to the barman, and Geraint's stomach flinches, waiting for the man to say something about the fridge, but all the man says is Goodbye.

Later, over gnocchi, he still doesn't feel right.

Niamh asks, Is everything okay?

Yeah, I'm fine, he says, I've just got this toothache. I think it's my wisdom tooth flaring.

That night, fooling around in bed, it takes a while for him to get hard. When he's hard enough, he pushes himself inside her, and he knows immediately – on the first catch of her breath – that he's going to come too soon. Hearing the change in her breathing, his arm around her, his face buried in her neck, a gate opens and it just rushes out of him. To cover, he keeps thrusting after he's come, he keeps going, but he can feel himself getting softer.

I'm gonna come, he finally says.

Not yet, Niamh pleads.

I'm sorry, he says, I'm coming, I'm coming.

Lying beside her he caresses her clit, but she's not that into it now. He knows she's frustrated with him.

I'm sorry I came so quick, he says. I was just really turned on.

Don't apologise, she says. You're not the first man it's ever happened to.

When she goes to the bathroom to pee, he lies there, his hand cupping his shrinking dick, his arm resting across the small mound of his belly.

*

The next morning, searching for the hotel laundry service, he finds himself entering a mirrored room, the door shutting closed behind him.

In the walls his face looks tired.

Captain Cumquick, the voice says.

Geraint reaches for the door handle but the door is locked.

I guess it's the beginning of the end now, the voice says. Your job is to please her, and if you can't do that, what good are you?

Geraint says nothing.

Look at your puny legs, the voice says. At home, your

skinny jeans flatter you, don't they? But here, when you're wearing shorts, my god! You look so pale and scrawny compared with all the other men.

Geraint pats his pocket and finds a key. He goes to open the door but finds himself sniffing the key instead. He runs it over his lips, licks it, and then, despite himself, but aware of what he's doing – he swallows it whole.

Yes, I think we'll keep you here a while yet, the voice says. But first, send in the driver.

*

Niamh is showering when the bus driver enters and flips Geraint over the table.

He pulls down Geraint's shorts and boxers and plunges his fingers inside his anus.

Roll back your foreskin, the driver commands.

Geraint shrieks as the driver disinterestedly inspects every last inch of him.

Get dressed, soft-dick.

Why are you doing this? Geraint says, shaking and sobbing.

The driver slaps him hard across the face.

Because you're nothing, the driver says. You're just a puny worthless piece of shit.

Geraint does not protest.

Alright there? Niamh says, her foot on the bed, drying her leg with a towel. Why didn't you join me in the shower?

*

On the stony beach in Hvar, a man is hiring out deck-chairs, but neither Geraint nor Niamh have the courage to approach and ask how much. They don't talk about it, he just knows that's what's going on. So they lie on their towels, the stones poking through, sticking into their backs. When Niamh wades into the sea, he stays put, looking after their bags. He has tried to learn to swim, but a friend half-drowned him for a joke at a party when he was six and he's still just too scared to give himself over to the water.

He watches her swimming out, moving further away.

He thinks: what the fuck is wrong with me?

Why can't he just go into a shop and ask for what he wants? Why is he so on edge at restaurants? Why can't he ask the man for a sun lounger? Why is he always on guard for a telling off? What is he so afraid of?

His world is shrinking and shrinking and all his body seems to say is, Please don't shout at me, I'm a good boy, I'm a good boy really.

Niamh is swimming, pushing out. She's never felt so far away, so distant. For a moment she disappears, she is gone, and it hurts, it's a real physical lurch – but just as sudden, she re-emerges, her head bobbing up above the water. What is she thinking?

He tries starting the book of Shirley Jackson stories he picked up at the airport, but the sun is too bright to read.

He thinks of his father, how he walked out on them – his mother, Geraint, his brother, and his sister – how he left them to rot in a rotting house. He thinks: his father wouldn't have done it if his own mother was still alive. After she died, everything was permissible.

He looks out to the sea, and Niamh is summoning him now. He gestures at their belongings, as if to say: *I can't leave this stuff here!* – but she urges him in with both hands.

So he heads towards the water, and she looks so lovely, standing in the waves. It's been nine months since they got together, and he can hardly believe that she is his person. Of all the people in the world, why does she love him? He's still starstruck by her mouth.

The water feels surprisingly pleasant, it's good to feel the resistance against his legs. He goes in a little further now, stopping just before the water reaches his waist, the buoyancy lapping inside of him.

She comes over smiling.

How is it? he asks.

So good, she says, and she puts her arms around him, and they hug each other tight, his arms clasped around her warm body, as they rock back and forth as if in a waltz, he and Niamh both grinning, laughing, the sunlight glinting off the sea.

*

Shaving now, it's his father's face in the mirror. He has his nose; and there's something about his own eyes he does not trust.

The door opens and the bus driver enters.

Take off your clothes, the driver says.

I won't do it, Geraint says, and the driver reaches for the truncheon.

Undress, he says again.

So Geraint removes his clothes. In the mirror, the shaving cream still on his face, he looks gaunt, the pockets under his eyes wet with tears.

Good boy, the driver says. Now pull off your face.

What?

Pull off your face and tear off all the skin on your body.

No.

Do it! Pull it all off, keep going and don't stop until you have revealed the real you.

What real me?

The small ugly you, the driver says. The wounded you, the wounded shrivelled charred tar-baby who fell in the well, who's sunk in oil, who's hardened and mossy, sunk in the pit of a body that all this time has gone around pretending to be you.

I don't know how, Geraint says

Well, you are going nowhere until you have done it, the driver says. Do you hear me? Do you? You you you you you.

*

In Pjaca Square the clock ticks down on their last evening of the holiday.

I think I could live here, Niamh says. It's calm. I can really hear myself think.

Me too, Geraint says.

*

You've opened something, Geraint. You tried to ignore it, cover it over, but it was always coming for you. And now you must dwell in this sorry place, where the tides are drawn by hostile moons.

*

Because you don't want to believe it's happening, you don't make a fuss.

You do not beat the doors and walls.

You do not scream or cry.

Your voice is not hoarse, your fists and knuckles will not bleed raw.

You just keep your head down, because you can no longer bear to see your own face in the mirror.

Day after day, you just lie on the floor, your legs spasming, your blood gurgling, your veins twitching, as wave after wave of something ancient passes through you.

*

Onboard the aircoach to Split airport, he worries. Inside his stomach he carries a cube. The cube contains waves of green light and hums at a low pitch. Inside the cube he's in a mirrored room, asking: why isn't the driver here yet? Where has he gone? The ticket man said the driver would be here by now.

He can see how it'll all go: the rushing off the bus, the running to departures, the shaking head of the woman behind the desk. He picks at the dry skin on his scalp, really digs his nail under.

Niamh cups his wrist and pulls his arm away.

Sorry, he says. I didn't realise I was doing it again.

We'll be there in plenty of time, she says.

And then looking out the window, she says: Goodbye Split, may we someday meet again.

By 8:10, there's still no one else on the bus and he wonders if they've been abandoned.

It is a bit odd, Niamh says, I grant you that.

At 8:15 a.m., a man opens the driver's door. He's heavy, has a tanned face. He's wearing a white shirt, top buttons undone, his chest hair curling out.

The driver, Geraint says.

Airport? the driver asks, looking at Geraint, weighing him up.

Yes, Niamh answers.

Good! the man says.

*

One day, the bus driver enters into the mirrored cube wearing a mask of your father's face.

He says: Why do you feel this way?

Why the mask? you say.

That's always a question worth asking, he replies. What do you think when you see me?

That I don't want to become you.

Well, I'm not your father, the driver says. And neither are you.

I don't know that I believe that.

Talk to me. What's going on in that little head of yours? What did you dream last night?

I dreamt again about the body buried under the floorboards. I think it was Niamh's—

Misplaced guilt and shame, the driver says. Look, you can't keep holding back. Shit or get off the pot.

I don't hold back, you say. I'm always there for her.

You just hide behind the support you give her, he says. It's just another way for you to not show up. Isn't that right?

I don't know.

Oh fuck off, the driver says. You're not even trying.

*

The bus pulls out of the station and now they're on their way.

Thirty-four degrees, Niamh says, looking at her phone. It's such a waste of sun. I wish it was like at restaurants when you can't eat everything on your plate. We should be able to box the leftovers and take it home.

133

Yeah, Geraint says, and then we could leave it in the fridge and completely forget about it until it goes off.

Niamh smiles and reviews the last week's worth of photos and videos. He hates looking at pictures of himself, but for her sake he turns his body towards her. She accepts the bid and tilts her phone, slowly swiping through memories.

The cat lying in the shade—

Geraint posing at the dock—

Stephen, the Austrian guy, making rock hands—

The quiet of Pjaca Square—

Niamh deletes the duplicates and the pics that fail to flatter. She double-taps Geraint eating gnocchi: a fork raised to his mouth, his eyes baggy, his teeth as terrible as ever.

That's an *awful* photo, he says.

She laughs. It's not the *best* photo of you I've ever seen. Delete?

Destroy, more like.

So into the bin he goes.

*

Over the years, your room fills with old cups of tea, scrunched-up tissue, plates with crumbs of toast. Stains appear on the ceiling. You begin to think of this mirrored cube as your room, the only room, the only place you'll ever live. The green light, the humming of the walls. There's no escaping yourself. In that mirror, it'll always be your sorry face.

You have moved so little in so long, your back tightens, your legs stiffen, and the bones in your arms are aching rods. Your muscles are shorter, weaker. But what is keeping you here? Why is this happening? Months pass and you ask the question again and again.

Until: It's *in* me! you yell one day at your image in the wall.

And then you say out loud: if I treated others the way I treat myself, I'd be in jail by now.

The light flickers.

Good boy, the voice says.

That night, the bus driver comes into the room with a pen, a piece of paper, and a CD player. His mask of your father's face is blotched with coffee stains and frayed at the ends.

I'm going to play you a track, he says. It's called 'Thawing'. I want you to just write. Don't think, just write. When I leave the room, hit play – and write.

The sound coming out of the player immediately plugs into the frequency of your pain. It's as if the music itself moves the pen across the page:

I was abducted by aliens, they did something to my insides, and I have never felt right since, it was a painful place to be, on the landing when they left me back that dark night, the smell of the wooden banisters, the flickering of the landing light, my mother was asleep, but there was smoke coming from her room, my sister was asleep my brother was asleep,

there was smoke coming from under the doors, the roof was caving in, the plaster was rubbling away beneath the peeling wallpaper, the ants and the spiders crawling over the paintpots in the kitchen under the little alcove, beneath the laundry beside the fridge, it was a Sunday night, the black bag of rubbish by the backdoor, it was dark and I came downstairs and I felt so alone, I was the only one downstairs and I was eight? Nine? I can't get over it, I can't forget what they did to me, they tore my insides out, their instruments were polished silver and cold and it did not hurt at the time, I just remember the cold, but I have never been right since, I have felt the absence, the loss of a vital organ that connected me with the world. In the days, weeks after I was drained in some vital way that no one seemed to notice. I craved sugar, I binged on biscuits and sunk gallons of sunny delight straight from the bottle, I was thirsty all the time and my skin was burning and my legs felt exhausted and my shoulder ached, I couldn't understand how my family did not realise I had been replaced with an imposter, and I still do not know where they put the real me.

When the music stops, the driver re-enters.

What on earth have I just done? you ask.

You don't know yet, the driver says.

In the mirrored wall, for a split moment, a child is staring back at you.

*

Along the dual carriageway, the starched-out grass is a haze of fuzzy yellow. Knowing now that they will make it to the airport in time, Geraint exhales, wraps his arm around Niamh, brings her close and kisses her on the cheek. Letting the breath out, he realises he's been holding onto it all morning, all holiday; he's been holding onto it since the day they got together.

You're my person, he says, and Niamh makes a contented sigh. She pockets her phone, then faintly, tiredly, rests her head against his shoulder.

He knows that if Niamh had asked her father for a lift, he'd have happily driven them back from the airport. But Geraint talked her out of it, said it wasn't worth the hassle. He couldn't get past a sequence of images in the scenario: her father standing beside his blue Audi in the airport car-park; then Niamh hugging him, and Geraint just to the side, holding the bags – looking gormless, feeling reproached for not being able to drive Niamh home himself.

He looks up. In the rear-view mirror, his father's eyes are watching. Niamh's head rests on his shoulder; she is dozing and he doesn't want to adjust his body in case she wakes. He thinks of the email he might write to her this evening when he gets home. He'll acknowledge all the ways he has worn her out this trip by being passive, all the ways he has sapped colour from her days.

He needs her to believe that he adores her, and he needs her to know that he's on the verge of something. He knows that she can't see it yet, but he can feel it. He wants to trust it, wants to stop fighting it. Because beneath all the pretending, deep down in the soil, something is asking, pleading, pushing through.

*

One afternoon, the bus driver wakes him from a deep sleep.

Shh, he says, and carries Geraint into another room, with windows with slatted blinds, and sunlight outside.

He has been in that place for years – or is it days? – and all that time he hadn't known there was an exit.

Why are you helping me? Geraint says. I thought you hated me.

The driver looks at him with genuine compassion.

Ah Geraint, the driver says. I never did or said anything you haven't thought yourself.

Oh, Geraint says.

Tell me, the driver says. What do you remember about being eight?

I remember after you left, Geraint says. I remember eating lunch in the canteen with my friends, how I felt marked out, apart from them.

I am not your father, the driver says. And neither are you.

I am not my father, Geraint says.

No, the driver says.

I think ever since I was a kid, I've felt this pressure to not fall apart.

Yes, the driver says.

With Niamh, I feel like it's my job to be stable. A lot of stuff in her life is mad, and she needs me to just—

Geraint slaps his hands together.

You know – be solid, not fall apart.

And be a proper man? the driver says.

I dunno, Geraint says. I don't know what that means.

Am I a proper man? the driver says.

Kind of? Geraint says.

What do you think when you see me?

I'm afraid of you, Geraint says. I'm afraid of most men.

Are you afraid of being a man yourself?

Oh god, I don't know. I don't know what I think.

Okay, the driver says. Let's come back to that. Let's try an exercise. Tell me the simplest truth.

Okay, Geraint says. When I was eight—

No, the driver says. Stay in the here and now.

I don't know how I feel, Geraint says. I never do. Not till months, years later.

You have to stay in the present tense, the driver says – and all evening he pushes and probes and pushes and probes, until late that night Geraint simply says:

I am hurt and I am sad.

He says: I want and need love, and it's gone on too long and something needs to change.

There's a beat of silence, and then the overhead light fizzes, buzzes, and explodes. The glass shatters everywhere, and the room is instantly dark.

*

He has consumed cocaine once in his life, eight years ago, but whenever he's in line for airport security he pictures nubs of coke nestled in the grooves and ridges of his ruck-sack. As his bag moves through the scanner, he catches himself mid-dread, picturing the bag abruptly turning down the bad conveyor belt – but no, it's all good, the bag is fine, no drugs have magically materialised between the hostel and the airport. He wants to laugh, at the relief of it, at his own ridiculousness.

Niamh is called forward: the security man gesturing with his hand. She walks through the X-ray machine no problem. Geraint smiles, and when he's called forward, he walks through the machine – and it beeps.

Please step aside, sir, the man says.

Raise your arms, sir, another voice, a woman's.

She looks Geraint in the eye and slowly presses the palms of her hands over his body. Niamh looks back and rolls her eyes, as if to say: My boyfriend!

Pockets? the woman asks.

In his pocket Geraint find a kuna, which the woman directs him to leave on the side table.

Go through again, she says, but there's a small queue now and so he stands behind two other passengers, just willing time to pass so he can emerge on the other side. Their cameras are trained on him; he can picture their zooming in: every tiny expression, every scratch of his temple, every lick of his dry lips.

Come through, a man finally says, and again the machine beeps, and then the bus driver bursts through, grabbing Geraint's collar and dragging him away.

Niamh looks on, her mouth open – but she does not seem, he thinks, at all surprised.

*

There are no days now, only nights.

Under torchlight, you keep talking, digging down, pulling truth from your innards, verbalising thoughts and feelings that scrunch your heart and flood your veins with heavy dread. After each session with the driver, your brain is a cauliflower on fire, the filaments lit and humming like the streetlights of Caerphilly at night. Your body is overwhelmed, it's a bath flooding over. But slowly, very slowly, you notice you are shrinking, receding, the false parts are falling away.

*

And then one day, on a morning that seems like all the others, you dare to say out loud: I think I'm ready to leave.

You think you're ready to leave, the bus driver says.

Yes I do.

Yes you do, the bus driver says.

Is that okay? Geraint says.

It's okay, the driver says.

A man comes in through the other door now. It jolts Geraint, he looks so much like him.

Leaving, are you? the man says.

You look like me, Geraint says.

I hope not, the man says.

Are you Welsh? Geraint says.

Oh, you still don't get it, do you? the driver says.

Get what? Geraint and the man say.

The driver shakes his head. It doesn't matter, he says.

Where's Niamh? Geraint says. Is she still here?

She's somewhere, the driver says.

What have you told her?

Nothing you haven't already, the man says. The usual shit that men always say: that you just needed some space to work things out.

We've been together a long time, Geraint says. I don't know where I've been for most of it.

You've been stuck, the man says.

She's waiting for me to push through myself, Geraint says.

She won't wait forever, the man says.

No, Geraint says. I have to go find her.

The driver quietly nods, and pushes the door open, and the light in the airport hallway is so bright that Geraint wonders how his eyes ever coped before.

As he waddles through the perfume store, the beautiful people gag and choke at his sight. They are repulsed by him, he is sure of it. Walking through the concourse, children point and laugh. He does not understand their words, but he knows what they're saying: they're telling their parents how disgusting he is, how vile, how small, how inhuman he seems. He is hurrying now, dodging past suitcases and baggage trolleys, crying all the while, his face so hot because of the moss that's risen over his neglected parts; the oil that's matted his fur. His tiny legs ache, the small balls of his calves are cramping with each step. Every few minutes he needs to stop to catch his breath, because his shrivelled walnut heart has never worked so hard.

At the moving walkway, he's afraid to step on. The belt is moving too fast to take the first step, so he goes the long way round, settling to the rhythm of his natural tread. When he finally reaches the farthest gate, and sees her, he stops. The hall is vast and tall and empty, and everything is quiet. Sat on the bench at the window, Niamh looks so small. Her feet don't reach the ground. She was once a child, and he can see that now as he stands at the doors, watching her sat there, deep in the bowels of the airport, waiting for him to arrive.

Birthday Teeth

With Mother ensconced in bed, I sit in the living room, with my eyes closed and my headphones on. Margaret is sleeping beside me on the couch and I am listening to 'Ave Maria', meditating, picturing myself at the dentist's tomorrow morning. The meditation is a new routine I'm attempting to foster during these night-time internet blackouts. Before Mother began cutting off the internet at 10 p.m., I would stay up until four or five in the morning, conversing with fellow vampires across the world. The dark hours are the ones in which I feel most myself. When the only sound is the thrum of the fridge and I am down-stairs alone; I am free to follow trails of thought and to venture down whichever avenues my mind discovers. In the light of the day, any thoughts I try to pursue are inter-rupted by Mother and her inane questions, or the constant murmur of the TV, or the terrible tumbling of the washing machine, and at evening by the manic noises of the wild youths who nightly congregate at the wall outside Cheng Wong's, whose patrons regularly see fit in disposing food cartons in our front garden, so that our wall and pathway are daily littered with burger trays and bits of chips.

I currently hold the position as a moderator on a major vampire forum. I mostly oversee discussions dedicated to philosophical enquiry. The arguments can sometimes become personal, and it is my job to remind our members of the Code of Conduct and to remove any content that is grossly offensive. I have learned not to expect kindness from others; I have learned that it is better to take before someone can take from you. It is difficult, because this isn't my nature – but my nature has never been good for me.

It is a little after eleven now and though I am far from tired – if anything, I can feel the green shoots of my mind waking, reaching out, awaiting nourishment – I should really try to sleep. Tomorrow I will leave early for the dentist. But an internet itch creeps under my skin. I want to check my mail, refresh the forum, be online and feel a part of something greater. So I do what I thought I wouldn't do: I get up and switch the router back on. When its three lights shine green, I once more look at the street-view for Mrs Sullivan's house: there it is, among a row of red-brick terrace houses, the occupants' cars neatly parked outside, their number plates blurred out. Tomorrow I will be inside that house, but if you looked it up on Google Earth, you would never know.

I refresh the forum for which I am responsible. Our members live across the world and post messages every minute of the day. There are a few hundred regulars, and I needn't spend much time surveying their posts, for they know the rules and they know I won't abide any misdemeanours. I click into a thread titled SOLIPSISTIC VAMPS, posted by a new user, but the page is slow to load – the progress bar is paused a quarter of the way through. I look up from the laptop and I see Mother in her pink dressing gown, the bread knife in one hand, the internet router in the other – its cords and wires severed and frayed.

Mother regularly tries to obstruct my access to her thoughts by thinking several different things at once. But now I hear her thinking only one thought: *no more, Glyn.*

My headphones are softly pulsing, a cello suite swirling gently inside my ear. I remove the headphones, and Mother and I stare at one another for some time.

'You—'

'I don't want to hear it,' she says, her voice quiet and clear. She turns then, and walks into the kitchen. She opens the bin and throws the router in.

'Oh my god,' I say. 'What on earth is wrong with you?'

'You never listen to me,' she says. 'But I've made my decision now. There'll be no more internet in this house.'

I push past her, to the bin, and reach in – through the malodorous food scrapings and eggshells and crisp packets – and retrieve the router, my sleeve and wrist getting wet in the process.

Mother's eyes are wide and vacant now, her lenses enlarged to let in the light. I break eye-contact before she can take something from me.

'You're not right in the head,' I say.

'Glyn,' she says. 'You'll be glad in the end, trust me. We don't need the internet in the house. And we don't want it either, not deep down. I really think it's making us ill.'

'Really?' I say. 'No more internet, is it? Well, how the hell are you going to do your online shopping? Don't tell me: you're going to call Tesco on the house phone and someone there will do it for you. Is that how it's going to work?'

'Oh,' she says. 'I didn't think of that.'

I tear the bedroom curtains off the rail and take bites at the skin around my wrist. Collapsed on the floor, I watch my chest rising, falling, filling. I am coming apart from the inside. The longer I remain me, the longer I remain here . . .

I have to get out. But I can't afford to move out yet.

I can't afford to live elsewhere.

By cutting those cables, she has cut me off from everything.

I get up and mount the wobble board. Breathing in deep, I hold my breath in at the abdomen for three beats, then exhale for seven seconds. I focus my senses inward, allowing the calm to build. I do this over and over, until I feel warm and tingling. I stand on the wobble board and search for calm in the blackness of my bedroom window.

Tomorrow I'll be twenty-one.

Tomorrow I'll have fangs.

I take the bunch of sage from my bedside drawer, open the window and put a match to the bunch. When the sage catches aflame, I quench it and smudge myself with the smoke.

I will not let that woman keep me down.

I will thrive to the capacity that I have within and outside of myself.

I remain on the wobble board for some time, meditating and repeating sacred mantras. Then I go to the kitchen and make three ham-and-cheese toasties which I eat in quick succession. In the kitchen window, I am clearly pale and in need of antioxidants. I eat three carrots and feel myself return, albeit only faintly.

Around 4 or 5 a.m., I am lowered into a state of lucid paralysis. I am a wooden table, and my mother is moving me around the house. She places me in the living room, then picks me up and carries me into the kitchen. A man enters and enquires about the table, and my mother replies that it isn't for sale, and the man says, Really? My mother thinks about it, smiles, and says, Well, how much are you offering? The man doesn't realise that I am electrified – but that's it, isn't it? Consciousness is just the murmur of electricity; my own consciousness can be put into anything. Before the sale is complete, my mother transfers my consciousness into the laptop; but no, it is more than that: I now *am* the laptop. The flashing green standby light is the pulse of my mind. She inserts a memory stick and I feel myself being downloaded onto the stick and then my mother ejects me from the laptop and carries me around the house. And though I guess it should feel strange to be carried around in that little cartridge, it all seems very normal.

*

In the kitchen, whisking away at some cream mix in a white bowl, Mother is adamant she doesn't remember cutting the router last night. She says she must have been sleepwalking again. I don't know whether to believe her, and I know better than to confront her about the consciousness-swapping.

'I was having such . . . strange dreams,' she says. 'You have to understand that, Glyn. The Wi-Fi, it honestly does weird things to my brain. You know I'm sensitive to stuff like that.'

My retinas are flaring, aching, struggling to take in the light. My circadian rhythm is inversed; I do not do well in the mornings. Mother speaks, and I feel weak but also distant, as if she is talking to me through a pane of glass.

Her theory, which she repeats slowly, so slowly, between sips of her chamomile tea, is this: her aura disrupts technology but is also susceptible to disruption by electrical waves.

I am without thoughts, and this is worrying. Has my brain been formatted? I recall some facts about myself, but I know that this could just be a trick. The brain is the hardware; the mind is the software. My brain could have been formatted, my old mind removed, and I could have been given new software, with some of the same old essential data – my memories, my sense of self – preloaded, but with my own programming, my own code, overwritten. And if this has happened, how would I ever know? True, there is comfort in the thought that this questioning might itself be an indication that I am still running the same consciousness, but again, maybe this doubt has been put there to make myself think I am still myself. But why would the programmer insert the doubt in the first place?

'But enough about last night,' Mother says, and she tilts the mixing bowl, pouring its off-white contents into a tin. 'What are you doing up so early? I was hoping to get this cake ready before you got up.'

She gestures at the tin, and I am annoyed with myself for not having a ready answer. I am sure I prepared a story yesterday. Then, almost unbidden, I say, 'I have a meeting at the Job Centre.'

'Oh Glyn,' she says.

'And afterwards, I'm visiting the agencies in town. I should be back by lunch.'

'That's very proactive of you,' she says. Then her face changes expression, becomes concerned. 'You should really give yourself a day off, though . . . On your birthday, at least.'

Five more minutes of Mother talking, and the back of my head will tighten, my heart will beat slower, pumping less blood around my body, and I will feel my face growing pale. Her slowness is draining. Each minute I spend in her company, my heart folds in on itself. I've recently undertaken protection measures. I visualise a mirror between us: a means of shielding myself from her negativity. I'm sure never to hold eye-contact for long, and when I'm looking at her, I just imagine seeing myself.

'Well, I'd best be off,' I say, and I walk to my room, retrieve the map print-outs, and head for the door.

'Wait . . .' Mother says. 'Can you give Margaret her injection? She's just had some food.'

I regard Margaret, her soporific visage, and slink back into the room and take the insulin kit from the cupboard. Margaret seems comfortable in my presence, and this is reassuring. Maybe I really still am the person I was yesterday.

I pass a treat beneath Margaret's nose, feel her teeth sharp against my fingers. I push the needle into her underside, stroke her neck and tell her she's a good friend.

'I'm leaving now,' I call.

'Okay, happy birthday, Glyn!' Mother answers.

'The same to you too,' I say, only realising, once outside, that this makes no sense at all.

It may be cold out – it is late October after all – but the world isn't touching me. I can see it, but I can't feel it. Maybe it's the new software, or maybe it's anticipation at what's to come – but as I walk through Caerphilly, past the tanning salon with the pumpkins wearing sunglasses in the window, past the gym with the bronzed muscle-bulging woman idling against the metal door, sipping a protein potion from a black sports bottle, and past the dismal red-brick hole that bears the misnomer of 'Job Centre', I feel as if my mind is a submarine, and my body is the waters it's travelling through.

It must be windy, because a wreath of poppies rises from the base of the cenotaph and floats in the air – floats,

floats – before dropping on its side and rolling across the road as a car pulls to a stop to allow the wreath to cross unhindered. But even as this is happening, it doesn't feel so much the result of wind, but rather a simulation, a visual relief designed by technicians. Maybe all of history is an invention too. The Second World War is just a Photoshop job.

There are times when my own past feels like a fiction, like something that didn't really happen to me. When I remember my childhood, what am I actually remembering? How is that little boy the same person I am now? I can't feel it, I can't feel that connection, so it's fair to presume we are different people, that I am not the self I think I am. Somewhere, somewhere, that little boy is still existing, he is still running up and down the stairs in the house, is putting floppy disks into the Amstrad, is playing games with terrible graphics. Maybe that's it; maybe the boy is a file stored away on a hard drive somewhere, one day I'll find the drive and I can plug it into a computer and open it up, open me up, and watch it all again, watch our family when my father was still alive, and my mother was still able to leave the house on her own. Would I be watching the game, or would I be in the game? And if I were in it, would I know I wasn't me, that I had just returned to play? How long would it take for me to forget that, to just re-enter that life and just be – to just live unselfconsciously, to just be in the moment, to just be the me that was me.

At Van Road, I stop a moment and listen, trying to hear the sounds beneath the drain, beneath the pavement. The cables for the internet lie underneath us, under our roads and fields. Along the bottom of the ocean, deep along the seabed, the cables cross thousands of kilometres, then rise up in cities, bursting through the concrete, plugging buildings and masts and people into the world. Sometimes, on quiet days, when I can still my mind and there is space between my thoughts, I can hear the swoosh, the movements of the waves.

It's cruel if we can never go back, if there isn't a way to access the life we had before. Nothing can be deleted, not really, not unless you take a hammer to it. Maybe someone took a hammer to my life after ten. Maybe that little boy is on a loop, he exists and he exists, and then the tape runs out, and he steps into a black void. He opens a door and the door opens to blackness, to space, and then he is no more. I don't really believe that, though. Someone on the forum wrote recently that it's a mistake to believe that there's a past and a future. They said everything has already happened. Or rather, everything, every moment, is happening all at once, but our minds aren't able to comprehend it because we don't have the hardware, so we're just standing in the dark, staring at one small spot on the ground lit by one small bulb, while all around us eternity is rushing past.

I walk through the bus terminal, the terminal that looks old and dated now. I remember when the station was new, when the green paint on the railings glistened like wet grass. But there I go again. Maybe this isn't a memory at all, maybe what I think is a memory is just a glimpse of the bus station as it exists elsewhere in another spacetime.

As I board the bus, the driver is eating an apple. With her mouth half-full, she says: 'Where you off to, love?'

'Pontypridd,' I say.

'Very nice,' she says. And then she takes another bite of her apple. 'Off to do a bit of shopping, are you?'

'Something like that,' I say, and I wonder how chewing will feel once I get my birthday teeth.

Despite her peaky complexion, it's obvious that this driver is a valuable source of psychic energy, so I sit as near to her as I can without raising suspicion: two seats from the front. Watching the passengers stream past me into the vacant seats, I am pleasantly surprised at how many others are joining us on this trip.

Out the window, sat at the benches under the bus shelter, an elderly couple share a packet of crisps, and an emotion surfaces in me, and my face begins to feel hot, and a space in my chest begins to thaw, and the fact of my being in the world is suddenly overwhelming. I have spent so much effort this last year not thinking about her, but sitting here, holding the ticket stub – the very same kind of ticket stub that she used to collect and keep in her wooden memory box – I feel the rush of all those feelings, and I do nothing to block them.

There we both are again, catching the bus, our fingers interlocked.

*

She was living with her mother in Germany when we first spoke. She listed classical music as an interest, and I reached out to her on MySpace. To my surprise and utter excitement, she replied and we began to discuss music and cinema, exchanging favourite songs and film clips. She introduced me to the works of Bach and Fritz Lang, and very quickly, the shape and length of the words 'Alice is typing . . .' became as familiar to me as the sound of my own voice. From the minute I arrived home from school to the minute I rested my head on the pillow, we conversed on MSN. We dined together, watched films together, and played games of online chess with one another.

Alice was by far the most intelligent person I had ever met, and I always felt compelled to try and impress her. Once, thinking that 'depraved' was the more intellectual form of 'deprived', I told her I'd had a 'depraved childhood'. An innocent mistake, but it opened up a realm of conversation that we'd both hitherto been too afraid to enter. Alice sent me links to forums and message boards, and then she sent me real books and real letters in the post. The thrill of seeing her handwriting for the first time – of seeing my name and address in her hand! Those German stamps – and her return address neatly boxed on the reverse side! Gradually, she initiated me into the workings of a psi-vamp's life, and for the first time in a long time I was able to step outside of the made-up self I'd been forced to construct all those years ago.

Amidst all this, Alice confided in me about her mother's cancer. I listened (or rather, I sat back and read as her messages filled the chat box) and tried to support her as best I could. Alice provided daily updates on her mother's condition – bad one day, worse the next, okay the day after – and she told me about their daily activities, like the first time they went shopping for wigs. I felt acutely the one-year age gap between us: I wasn't as mature as her and I didn't know the things she knew. So I told Alice about my father's death, and how in the following years I became Mother's 'alarm clock' because she was prone to sleeping in till noon; and how I used to do the food shops alone when Mother couldn't face leaving the house. I told Alice details about my home life that I hadn't shared with anyone, and when I felt Alice was beyond my reach in some nuanced feeling of despair, I would exaggerate and invent feelings I never actually felt about my father's death.

I read that people dealing with grief spend so much time needing to lean on others that it can come as a relief for them to be perceived as someone strong enough to be leaned on themselves. So I invented sadnesses and exposed vulnerable feelings that didn't exist. But once I told Alice these things, I began to believe them about myself; they became a part of my own personal narrative. It made me wonder if being able to invent a feeling was, in some way, evidence of always having had the feeling. But there were times when Alice would write such long, detailed, and knotted paragraphs, and I wouldn't know how to reply. She once filled the chat window with a description about the way she'd have to turn the TV off each night as her mother dozed in front of it, and how the action filled her with a sadness she couldn't bear. She didn't know how she and her mother should be spending their time together now they knew it would soon come to an end. It made her wonder what life was for, what her own life was for. Thinking to the future, any major hopes or ambitious life projects just felt banal and worthless. And yet the small things, the things that were meant to make up a life, make it meaningful, felt equally pointless. Would her mother really spend the last days of her life watching TV with her daughter?

At times like these, it felt like I had reached a wall, a wall I wasn't smart enough or mature enough to climb. I would write out a message, and then delete it. And then, after a minute of anxious thinking – my fingers hovering and flailing over the keys – I would just say sorry and apologise for not knowing what to say. This must have happened at least ten times. And on at least ten occasions, Alice assured me that I needn't say anything, that my listening, my being online, was enough.

Two years into our relationship, when I was enrolled at the University of Glamorgan studying Computer Science, Alice messaged to say her mother had died – and could we Skype? I was in the university computer room, and that evening we put our hands to the screen so that they were touching. Sitting there, among the other students as they wrote their essays, I cried with Alice, and watched as her face became something else: lost and raw, but also somehow wiser, more knowing. After the funeral, I used the remainder of my student overdraft to pay for her plane ticket to Cardiff. From the moment we sat on the bus into town, it was clear to us that her stay would be permanent.

Mother took to Alice immediately, and they spent a lot of time together, without me, which came as a great relief. Shortly after my father died, my mother found it hard to leave the house. I was ten at the time and I didn't understand what was happening. At first I just thought it was funny: I would stand on the pavement outside and wave at her through the window. But her anxiety got worse and eventually she refused to go outside on her own. She just physically couldn't do it. The furthest she ever reached was the lamppost four houses down.

The doctors tried many things, and Mother was prescribed all kinds of medicines and was even hypnotised once, but nothing succeeded in keeping her panic at bay once she left the house. She said it felt like choking, like dying. So from the age of ten, I became my mother's bodyguard, accompanying her everywhere – medical appointments, the hairdresser's, the DSS. It's still the same now. My aunt helps, taking her out once or twice a week, and driving us to the supermarket for the big shop on the weekend. And my uncle, when he was still alive, came by whenever he could. But mostly, it's just me. Even when I am on my own, I don't feel free of her: I keep checking my phone in case she needs something. So having Alice with us made life easier – and lifted a heavy burden from my chest.

While I was at college lectures, Alice and Mother would go out on little trips. Alice even got Mother all the way to

Cardiff on the train, something I had never been able to do. I remember coming home and the two of them drinking tea on the couch. Mother was delighted with herself, shopping bags at her feet, the two of them laughing as they compared their hauls. Another time I came back from college and found them giddy and excited, with sheets of paper laid out all over the carpet. They had been watching a programme about children with autism and they'd now concocted the perfect business plan: selling seamless socks to the families with autistic children who couldn't wear socks with seams. That evening Alice set up the eBay account, and the house soon filled with packets of socks and padded envelopes. She found a cheap supplier in Italy, and that was that: she could buy a pack of three pairs of seamless socks for €5 and sell them online for £20. The business was slow to take off, but our trips to the post office soon became more regular, and the boxes we carried grew heavier, until we were daily taking two boxes to the post office – boxes full of seamless socks, which we were sending all across the country. For the first time since my childhood, our fridge was no longer empty; it bulged with food and colour.

With Alice living with us, I found I wanted to kill Mother less often. It helped, of course, that we finally had some income other than the state allowances, but more than that, the air in the house somehow seemed lighter with Alice in it: it was as if the ceilings were raised to accommodate her. There were still times when Mother would do or say something annoying, and I would vent about it to Alice, but Alice made me look at things from a different perspective. It was peculiar, but I found that I could see Mother differently if I really made the effort. I could interpret her behaviour as a result of her anxieties, and not as part of her personality. If I paused before reacting to something she said, I could choose to understand her clinginess as a fear of being left behind, and I could respond with care as opposed to just leaving the room. But seeing the control I had over my own responses made me uneasy. If I could just change the way I thought about something or someone, well, who or what was I? What did I really believe? What did I *really* think?

When myself and Alice and Mother were in the same room, I felt two versions of myself coming into conflict: I was Glyn the son, but I was also the Glyn I had been presenting to Alice. There were times when the latter version slipped, and when I was Glyn the son in Alice's presence I saw myself through Alice's eyes, and my pettiness and childishness would embarrass me, and I would feel the need to alter myself. Sometimes, when Alice wasn't there, I could maintain this new way of being towards Mother; but then on other occasions I found myself being doubly cruel to Mother – being abrupt with her, dismissive, mocking – as if to punish her for being a witness to how inauthentic I was.

My whole life, I had wrestled with these ideas of self and, most acutely, with the very plain fact that I felt like a different person when I was with different people. I was not constant. But Alice was adamant that this was wrong-headed. She explained that in the same way the earth has an atmosphere, we each of us have an atmosphere, too – an etheric body. When we come into contact with different atmospheres, it can change us: some etheric bodies are more powerful than others, and can drag us into their gravitational pull, while others move away from us and we go chasing them for fear of being left abandoned in space; and sometimes we encounter people who strip us of everything: they puncture holes in our ozone, and they destroy our atmosphere, disrupt our magnetic poles. If we're not careful around these people, if we don't take precautions, our sense of gravity goes haywire and our planet becomes inhospitable.

The aim, she said, was to harness all the energy we encountered in order to strengthen our true selves. She told me to not see these different parts of myself as separate selves, but different perspectives and responses which emerged from the whole. Through certain physical exercises that she taught me, I began to see the outline of my etheric body reflected in the bedroom window: a fuzzy grey border that in her company seemed to pulse.

It would be dishonest to say something along the lines of: 'times were good then', because I felt, for the first time in my life, as if I were fully awake each day in such a way that makes it hard to group all those times together. I was fully present, and in tune with my body, my thoughts, and my emotional weather. Alice sorted out my diet so that I no longer binged at night, so that each plate of food I ate contained a rich variety of colour. I lost weight and felt so much better for it.

At some point, I observed that Alice had inherited a cough from Mother. It was smaller, less throaty, but it shared an auditory resemblance. Occasionally I would return from college and she and Mother would both be nursing headaches, or they'd both be in bed, the two of them reporting similar complaints. I put it down to them spending so much time together, picking up small bugs from one another, and though I sensed that something was amiss, I couldn't tell from which direction the flow of energy between the two was moving. I did, however, suspect that Mother was to blame. But I noted it and then ignored it, the way you might pick up some gut feeling about a character at the start of a film but don't keep it in mind.

But with Alice beside me, it was as if the brightness dial had been turned up: my image of the world and everything in it grew firmer and sharper. Meanwhile, the boys who nightly gathered at the wall between the church and Cheng Wong's no longer called me a faggot or mocked my hair or my leather coat. The first time Alice and I walked hand in hand, Margaret tugging at the lead, we received a chant of: 'You're goths and you know you are!' to which Alice smirked and responded – using the same sing-song tune – 'You're virgins and you wank too much' and the boys laughed, applauded her reply, and thereafter they more or less left us alone.

Mine and Alice's lives grew entwined, but after six months Alice still sensed there was some block between

us. I felt it was to do with the intercourse: it was difficult to have it, what with Mother always being around. It
wasn't so much that I was embarrassed or inhibited, but I
could tell that there were things we weren't doing because
Alice didn't want Mother to hear. Yet Alice was adamant
that no, it wasn't that – and she suggested we try something she had read about online.

'It's called Radical Honesty,' she said, and she showed
me articles about the concept. 'The goal is to be honest,
completely honest, about everything all the time. And then
instead of presenting our false selves, we will present our
true selves, and then we can achieve a deeper, more meaningful intimacy.'

We started with little confessions: she thought I squeezed
too much toothpaste onto my brush ('but maybe it's a
British thing?') and I said I thought there were times she
pretended she was tired so that we wouldn't have sex. She
said that she worried that the many fillings I had might
cause her teeth to rot when we kissed, and she asked that
in future I take better care of my dental hygiene. I told her
she was stingy with compliments.

'Do you want me to tell you you're beautiful?' she
asked, kind of mocking.

'Well, yes,' I replied.

We told each other things we had been afraid to tell
ourselves, let alone one another: Alice admitted to feeling
relief when her mother finally died; I said I was sometimes
glad I no longer had a father because only having one parent meant I had more freedom. The honesty became a kind

of game for us, and very soon we began seriously talking about bloodletting. Alice confessed she had tried it once years ago with an ex-boyfriend, and she had been drawn to the idea ever since, but she had been waiting to meet the right person. She described this confession as coming out of the coffin.

We read all the material we could find – pages and pages of websites with black backgrounds and white text, which left our eyes dizzy. Each blog and article emphasised the same thing: the importance of clinical testing. If a person is anaemic, for example, losing too much blood can make them ill. There are risks of infection, of hepatitis. The donor might have kidney disease, undetected diabetes. Neither of us could face the idea of going to the doctor's for tests, so the next day – a summer's afternoon, the two of us sweltering in our leather jackets, and donning our matching Ray-Bans, afforded thanks to the now-booming trade in seamless socks – we walked to the blood bank: the large lorry hitched in the Asda car park. On seeing us approach, the woman at the lorry laughed and said: 'Mr and Mrs Dracula! You're not here to steal the blood, are you?'

We smiled and offered our arms in return for two Kit-Kats. A fortnight later we received two letters: mine saying that my blood was good, Alice's saying that she was anaemic.

In the darkness of my bedroom, we started small: lancets on the tip of my finger. There wasn't much blood but Alice sucked like her life depended on it, and the first time it was all so much that we just had to make love immediately, Alice sucking my finger until I came so hard inside her.

We soon turned to razor blades, sterilising them with boiling water that Alice carried into the bedroom in a bowl. Alice suggested that she make an X mark with the blade, as opposed to just one cut. She said it would put less pressure on the spot where she sucked the blood. She took the blade and carved a cross into the back of my shoulder. It felt so good to give myself to her like that, to see the pleasure she got from it. But she rapidly became demanding and wanted to cut me almost every day. One day I responded – in her view – without sufficient enthusiasm, and she accused me of not being into the idea as much as her – and that maybe I was just doing it all to please her.

'There's just no real bite in you,' she said.

'There is!' I insisted.

'It's just so unattractive when you just go along with things. I want you to be the real you, to be fully confident enough to be your own person and go your own way.'

She was right, of course, but the comment still angered me, and that evening when we were fooling around on the bed, I bit her shoulder with such force that she let out a scream so loud that Mother came running to the bedroom door.

'It's okay, it's okay,' Alice reassured her through the door. 'We were just watching a scary film.' And then she turned to me and smiled, running her fingers over her shoulder, the blood streaking.

'Taste me,' she said, and I put my lips to her wound.

Over the next twenty-four hours I felt revitalised in ways I never imagined. I had become like her, and I saw that with more aggression, with more directness, I could get on with life. The next evening, when I was lying on the bed, post-intercourse, listening contentedly to the sound of Alice showering, her mobile rang, and I leaned over and saw the name: Elke.

I answered, and the voice, a foreign voice, on the other end said: 'Alice?'

'No,' I said, 'who is this?'

And the voice said: 'Elke. I am Alice's mother. Is Alice with you?'

It was as if a plug was pulled, like with a TV, when you pull out the plug and the sound goes, and the image shrinks to the centre then collapses, and the screen is black and there's no sound except the fading aftermath of sound. Alice left the next morning.

The bus's muggy heating is making me feel rather faint now. My throat feels stuffy with stale arm air. We pass over a speedbump and a few fellow passengers make a 'wuh' sound, and my stomach lurches. I close my eyes and picture the etheric cord beginning from me and passing through the air, through the driver's cabin, right through into her chest. I badly need energy, and I know I won't be able to stop myself from taking everything. I can see the cord in front of me: it's like the water spout my father and

I saw on the beach in Porthcawl, when the cloud over the sea sucked the water right up. When I took the photo into school I was almost popular for a day.

Since I was little, I have operated under the belief that there is something wrong with me. I've pictured organs rotting, devouring me from the inside. Despite my fear of hospitals, I have fantasised about visits to a clinic, about tests being run, and a group of doctors with clipboards excitedly gathering around me, saying, 'This is remarkable. We can't believe you've achieved so much when you've been labouring under such health difficulties. You have basically been running at only 12 per cent capacity. Now that we've identified the problem, we can cure you of your ills, and you will be unstoppable!'

At Glamorgan, I watched as the other students handed in assignments, held down jobs, learned to drive, ran marathons, posted photos of them and their partners looking healthy at terraced restaurants in Mediterranean towns, while I lurked in the dark, unable to understand how I would ever muster the requisite spirit to leave the house. I stopped going to class, and I lost the ability to focus on coursework, and when exams came round and it was time to revise, I couldn't bear to face the sum of what I didn't know. In the summer, when my tutor emailed asking to meet, I couldn't reply. I can't even say now that I 'dropped out' – because that phrase implies being active in some kind of way. Whereas I did nothing; I just became mouldy.

During this time, Alice sent me so many emails, pleading, apologising, saying that before she met me she had been unwell, but that I had saved her, changed her life. She told me she hadn't been lying about her mother's cancer – but that it had all happened a few years before, and her mother had survived. She was still trying to work out why she had lied about it. She proposed many reasons, claimed all kinds of insecurities. I had several theories of my own, and I wrote replies, detailing all these ideas, but I never sent any of them. I just didn't know what to believe, and I didn't know who to believe – Alice or myself – and I realised that in the end our theories were just stories, and our reasons for choosing one theory over another would have nothing to do with the truth; we would just believe the story we wanted to believe, the story which said about us the things we wanted to hear. I still missed her, and I wanted to forgive her. Though some days I just wanted to sever the tie entirely – to tell her never to write to me ever again – because every time I opened a new email from her, it was as if she were still yielding a force over me, piping the life out of my limbs. I decided not to reply at all, and eventually her emails stopped.

After that, I tried ignoring and giving up who I was. Being myself had brought me so much pain, I thought it best to become a new me, to try and be like the others. So I tried going to bed before twelve, I tried waking up before noon, I tried enjoying the TV shows my mother watched, I tried dressing normally, tried reading current affairs, tried drinking alcohol in regular establishments, tried smiling and politely exchanging interesting and interested remarks with other dog-walkers, tried tapping my foot to the songs that played on the radio, and I tried believing that this kind of life could contain me, could satisfy my needs.

But I did all this, and nothing changed.

Because some things are in the blood, and I know my blood is unlike theirs. Like this bus driver – for all that she's pale, she has within her the power and the resources to control this vehicle. I, alone, could never make it move.

And so I take from her.

But I've never made anything so visible as this etheric cord; surely the other passengers can see it now. The energy is astonishing: it feels like I'm downloading straight from the driver, directly into myself. Alice loved doing this on buses, though shopping centres were her favourite – because there were so many people, so many sources of energy.

The driver's shoulder begins to jerk and the bus takes a few hops. I know I have to stop, but I can't. I have to take everything from her. We're at Nantgarw now, near the cinema, and the bus is pulling over and the driver stumbles out of her seat, and out the door, and I watch through the window as she vomits into a bush.

When she stumbles back onto the bus, her face is white, and she is shaking her head.

'I'm not being funny, but I think I've got food poisoning.'

She tells us there is another bus on its way, but I cannot wait now, I am restless with life, so I walk the remaining two miles, occasionally skipping, and then calming down before I bring undue attention upon myself.

By the time I reach Pontypridd I am starving. The gush of energy from the driver – though sensational – is not nourishing in the same way as food. In the Spar I stalk the aisles and find a cherry-glazed flapjack.

But what a bad impression that would make on the dentist, to bring in teeth coated and wedged with oats! And yet it could be hours until I eat again after the procedure. So I buy the flapjack, a pack of two tooth-brushes (the smallest pack available), and a tube of pearly white Colgate toothpaste, and a 500ml bottle of water. I wouldn't ordinarily spend money so freely, but since I started selling the seamless socks again, I have allowed myself a little discretionary spending.

I put the spare toothbrush in my coat pocket, and eat the flapjack in three bites. I can feel the oats lodged there, between my teeth. I walk around the town, and finally find a quiet lane, which backs onto the rear of an office block. The lane is peaceful, and I hear only the sounds of birds whose names I don't know. In a few hours' time I'll have fangs, and I'll be tuned into new frequencies.

Facing a wall, I brush my teeth and gargle, frantically, afraid of being caught by someone. I do not know why, but brushing my teeth in this lane feels like the act of a degenerate; it seems indecent, illegal. I have no problem flouting societal values, but I am deeply fearful of the law and figures of authority. In public parks with Alice, I always insisted we left in good time before the official closing; on trains I am anxious and restless until the con-ductor has confirmed my ticket is valid.

Hearing close by the sound of heels and laughter, I throw the toothbrush over my shoulder and stride away, my scalp prickling under my hair.

Approaching the dentist's, I feel a twitching inside, like something is trying to climb out. The street, the trees, and the house itself look exactly as they do on Google Maps; and as I open the gate I feel as I've been here before. My brain fidgets and I picture a dank, grey chamber, a steel casket; and from the casket a series of umbilical cables plugged into a large computer server. Breathing in deep, I hold my breath in at the abdomen for three beats, then exhale for seven seconds. I focus my senses inward, allowing the calm to build. I do this a few times, until I feel warm and tingling.

The man from the forum said that Mrs Sullivan was a little odd, but that she was ultimately someone our kind could trust. Either way, she is the only dentist in the area who's willing to perform the procedure. I step forward and ring the bell. In her window she has a 'Vote Green Party' sign. I wipe the sweat from my face and wait.

The glass in the door darkens, and the door opens, and there she is: small and wrinkled, she looks like she could be somebody's grandmother. She's wearing a green cardigan with a purple brooch.

'You must be Glyn!' Mrs Sullivan says. 'I'm Deepti. What a beautiful jacket! Come in, come in!'

The floor tiles are orange; in front of me is a wooden staircase. She takes me through to the kitchen, and asks if I would like a drink. She herself is drinking some kind of herbal tea, and she gestures at the tall glass on the counter, steam rising from its honeyed liquid.

'I am okay, thank you,' I say.

'I can tell you're okay,' she says. 'I was just asking if you wanted a drink.'

A thin smile breaks on her lips and then she casts her head back and starts laughing very hard. I stand there doing nothing, because I refuse to laugh unless I know what the joke is.

'Please,' she says, 'do sit down.'

I take a seat at the high counter, and survey the kitchen, feeling myself shrink in the presence of a home so much nicer than my own.

'I have the money,' I say. 'Do I pay you now?'

'Oh that can wait.'

'Okay, but I do have it.'

Her face is open, interested.

'So you've come from Caerphilly today?' she says, nodding as she waits for my answer.

'Yes,' I say. 'I took the bus.'

'Can you not drive?' she says.

'I can't,' I say.

'Ooh, you should really learn,' she says. 'It's a very good life skill.'

'I don't have much interest in it.'

'No?'

'I think too much,' I say. 'I'd be a danger to myself and others if I was behind a wheel.'

'Well, I don't even have the energy to think any more,'

she says, and then she laughs again. 'I've done sixty-seven years of thinking and it's left me worn out. Are you living at home then?'

'I am,' I say.

'And do your parents know you're here today?'

'No,' I say. 'And it's just my mother.'

'Oh right,' she says.

'My father died when I was young.'

'I'm so sorry,' she says. 'That's awful. It must have been very hard for you and your mother.'

'These things happen,' I say.

Most people have terrible instincts about other people. I, however, have learned how to read others, to see through the surface, right through to who people are. And Deepti Sullivan has a good energy about her. Aside from the £120 sealed in the envelope in my coat pocket, she isn't looking to take anything from me.

She takes a few sips of tea, then sets the cup down on the counter. My mind plays a memory of Mother, in those weeks and months after my father died, when she barely left the couch, and teacups collected around her on the floor.

'How long have you been a vampire then?' Mrs Sullivan says. 'I should probably tell you: my boy was a vampire too.'

'Is he dead?'

'Not quite,' she says, 'he's an accountant.'

'I suppose I have always been a vampire,' I say. 'Though it's been four years since I knew I was, if that makes sense.'

'It does,' she says. 'I was always a dentist really, but it took me a long while to realise that's what I was.'

'It's a bit different,' I say.

'Of course,' she says. 'I just meant, well, we all have things we need to do and it's good when we do them. Speaking of which. Those teeth of yours. It wouldn't be right if I didn't ask again: are you *sure* that you can't be persuaded go with veneers? As I said in one of the emails, I could attach the veneers to the canines, no bother. And they have the advantage of not being permanent, you know?'

'No,' I say. 'I want them sharpened. I want them to be real.'

'Very well,' she says, 'I can tell you're a man who knows his own mind. My Rory was the same. Once he had his heart set on something, that was it. As soon as he decided he wanted fangs, he was at me all the time about it. Actually, let me show you some of my handiwork.'

From a shelf beside the cooker, she takes down a black book and hands it to me. It's a photo album. I flip through the pages, focusing intently on the many close-ups of mouths with fangs.

'So what do you think of them then?' she says, and she's clearly happy with her portfolio, and well she should be.

She talks me through different options, different styles. She tells me stories about previous vampires she's worked on, how they're always far politer and more thankful and gracious than the other patients she sees. Listening to her,

I feel strangely proud of our kind, but I also feel like an imposter. All the vampires I talk to are living abroad. I don't socialise with the vampires in South Wales – I haven't yet felt able to go to the socials and the gatherings, and besides, I don't really like parties. It's a peculiar thing – feeling part of a group you're not physically with.

The dentist finishes her tea, then asks if I have any allergies.

'I'm not good with dairy,' I say.

'Dairy?' she says.

'Yes,' I say, 'milk makes me sneeze. Full-fat milk especially.'

'Milk? Bloody hell. I meant medicinal allergies, Glyn. You know, like penicillin.'

'Oh,' I say. 'No, I have no medicinal allergies. Or rather, none that I know of.'

'Well, that's all good then,' she says. 'Now, I know I don't need to remind you, and I'm sorry to bring it up, but for my own sake, for my own piece of mind, I do have to say: please keep today's visit confidential. You understand, I could get struck off for doing this kind of business.'

'Of course,' I say.

'Thank you,' she says. 'I always hate having to say that bit. It makes the whole thing seem . . . shameful, when it really shouldn't be. I know you might tell other vamps about it . . . and that's all good so long as you know they're legit, but I can't be doing with a string of people turning up at the door. God knows what the neighbours already think.'

'I won't tell anyone,' I say. And I think: it's not like I've got anyone to tell about it anyway.

The dentist smiles and nods her head, and I have to stop myself from nodding in return. In social interactions, many people mirror the person they're talking to; it seems like a natural instinct, but if you want to remain yourself, if you want to remain you, you mustn't get swept up in other people's currents.

My stillness changes her somewhat; I can see it in her body language. She claps her hands together, then says: 'Well, those teeth aren't going to sharpen themselves, Glyn. If you're ready, I'm ready. Are you ready?'

'I am,' I say.

'Excellent,' she says. 'Let's go make you some fangs.'

As I get up off the chair, she says, 'Oh, you can leave your coat here.'

'I'd rather keep it on,' I say.

She laughs.

'As you wish,' she says.

I follow her to a door at the back of the kitchen, and she brings me down a wooden staircase. The basement is well lit and a radio is playing. She instructs me to get onto the dentist chair, then ties a green bib around my neck.

'When were you last at a dentist?' she asks.

'A long time ago,' I say. 'Possibly six or seven years. Yes, I think I was fourteen at the time.'

'That is quite a while,' she says. 'Are you experiencing any problems with your teeth or gums? Any sensitivity or pain when you eat or drink?'

'Sometimes,' I say, 'but I have learned to eat on one side of my mouth.'

'That doesn't sound like fun,' she says.

'It is what it is,' I say.

She smiles, though the smile seems almost sad. She says: 'Well, I suppose everyone bears pain differently.'

She lowers my chair, leans in, and inspects my mouth. No one has been this close to my teeth since Alice. The dentist is in there now, with her little mirror, inspecting whatever horrors lurk inside. I think of Alice again, of her fear that my own teeth would cause her perfect teeth to rot.

'Can you smile for me, please?' the dentist says, leaning forward. 'Teeth together now.'

She stands up straight to look down on me.

'Glyn Morgan, that is not a smile.'

I try again to smile, and she shakes her head.

'Do you not know how to smile?'

'I might be out of practice,' I say.

'Well, if you won't smile for me, I refuse to continue with the procedure.'

She leans back over, and I try my best to smile, and she laughs, and says, 'That's better.' Then she instructs me to open up again, and reaches her mirror into my mouth, tutting as she moves the mirror from tooth to tooth.

'I'm just going to sit you back up now,' she says. 'And I'm afraid this next part might put an end to your career in smiling. Do you want the bad news or the really bad news?'

'I'll take both,' I say.

She tells me I need five fillings and probably a root canal. There's also a wisdom tooth coming through that needs attention.

'In all good conscience,' she says, 'I just don't know if I can do this procedure when you have so many . . . well, so many other problems.'

'You're joking,' I say.

'I wish I was, Glyn. There are *holes* in your teeth, and some of your old fillings need repairing. I can book you in for another appointment soon,' she says. 'But it wouldn't be right to let you leave here with your teeth in that state.'

'Oh come on,' I say, and I hear something break in my voice. I sound on the verge of tears. 'Please,' I say. 'Please do it.'

'I'm just not sure if it's the best idea,' she says.

'You have to sharpen my teeth,' I say.

'There are so many other problems in your mouth, Glyn.'

'Sharpen my teeth,' I say, my volume rising. Then I feel a surge inside me, growing. 'Sharpen my teeth or I'll *kill* myself.'

'Glyn!' she says.

'I will,' I say, and I get up off the chair, and I point to the wooden floor. 'I'll do it here and you'll have to deal with the body and explain to everyone what I was doing here in the first place.'

'Glyn,' she says. 'Calm down. Please. Sit down.'

'No!' I say. 'You have to do this for me, I need it.'

'Take it easy,' she says. 'It's okay.'

I realise that I may have overreacted. I sit back down on the chair. 'I've just been waiting a long time for this,' I say, and I push the hair out of my eyes.

'I understand,' she says. 'And look, if that's what you really want, we can do it today, okay? We can sharpen your teeth. Though I'll need to book you in for a follow-up. But no one's going to kill themselves today, okay?'

I'm silent a moment. I feel a beating in my chest, a strain across my collarbone. 'Thank you,' I say. 'You have no idea what this means.'

'It's okay,' she says. 'But you shouldn't go around making threats like that.'

'You're right,' I say. 'I didn't mean it. I'm sorry.'

'Are you okay now?' she says. 'Do you need some time to calm?'

'I'm okay,' I say.

'Good,' she says. 'Right. Okay. You've made me a bit flustered now, though. I think I need a slice of toast.'

'Okay,' I say. Then: 'Wait, did you say toast?'

'Yes, I'll just be a minute.'

I lie in the chair as the dentist walks back up the stairs. I go through my breathing exercises, attempting to come to some peace. For a moment, I picture stabbing myself, collapsing on the floor, my blood staining my shirt. I imagine a hoover then; I imagine the hoover in my head, hoovering up the thoughts and the images, until my mental screen goes black.

In an hour's time, I'll be walking the streets with fangs. There's something almost unsettling about the thought

– about being so close to what I want. When Alice first moved over, I told her how being with her made me feel so happy, so achieved, that I was starting to feel anxious when crossing roads. I would look one way then the other, two, three, four times, before I would cross. I was convinced that because something good had happened to me, that the good thing was bound to get cancelled out, that I was sure to be knocked over and killed.

Mrs Sullivan returns, carrying a plate with a slice of toast in one hand, and a sheet of kitchen towel in the other. I can smell Marmite. It makes me think of my mother.

'Do excuse me, Glyn,' she says, 'but you really gave me a shock with all that talk of killing yourself.'

'I'm sorry, I was being over the top,' I say. 'My mother has always said I'm prone to dramatic gestures.'

Mrs Sullivan nods, then takes a bite of her toast.

'There's a lot of iron in Marmite,' she says, chewing. 'I recommend it if you're ever in need of a boost after a shock.'

She continues to eat, and I watch her chew. During my teenage years, when my limbs felt so heavy, I became convinced there was a giant magnet at the centre of the earth pulling and dragging down the iron in my blood. I felt slow and tired all the time, so I gorged on cakes and crisps for some kind of boost. Mother never cooked. She lived on Marmite and toast. But my body was a landfill and I gorged on cakes and crisps. My body was a landfill and it needed trash to burn.

I can't bear thinking about those dark afternoons, when I'd arrive home from school heavy-legged and go straight to my room. I hadn't yet mastered how to do up a tie, so I would gently loosen it off and hang it on the bedpost, ready to re-noose myself the next morning, and by Friday the knot would be so small and so tight – and that's how I felt sitting on the couch each evening, wearing my school trousers and shirt, the TV washing over me and my mother as the sky turned to tar and the house shrunk around us – I felt I *was* the knot in my tie, and I was convinced I would never again feel loose of myself.

When she's done eating, Mrs Sullivan wipes the crumbs off her hands in the kitchen towel. 'Actually,' she says, 'I'd best go wash the smell off.'

I lie there, eyes closed, and hoover away the image of me as a teenage boy. When Mrs Sullivan returns, I feel it inside me, running in my blood – I am ready for my fangs.

'Okay,' she says. 'First things first. We need to numb your mouth. What are you like with needles?'

'I'm good with them,' I say. 'My dog has diabetes, so I inject her every day.'

'Excellent,' she says. 'Well, not for the dog. But you know what I mean.'

She takes a needle from a transparent case, and then I decide to stop watching and just let my fate unfold. I lie back and wait for the needle to pierce my gums. When it's done she gives me a cotton swab, and asks me to hold it there, between my gums and lips.

'It'll only be a few minutes for that to take effect,' she says. I can already feel I'm losing sensation.

She walks across the room, though I can't see where

she's going. I hear a rattle, then she returns with a Cadbury's Christmas biscuit tin. Why does the dentist have a biscuit tin?

With my hand in my mouth, keeping the cotton wool at my gum, my gum which is starting to disappear from my order of senses, I mumble, 'Whatsgoingon?'

'Everything's okay,' she says, and she opens the tin and extracts a Discman and a pair of headphones.

I look up at her.

'It's just a bit of music,' she says. 'For the procedure, I'm going to give you a little bit of gas, and the music will help you relax.'

'Gas?'

'I did mention it in the emails,' she says, and she puts the headphones into my ears and the Discman in my hands. She turns it on, hits play, then gives me the thumbs-up.

She attaches a grey mask across my nose, then the music begins, a humming of voices, like a buzzing of tuneful bees, and then a man's voice singing forlornly:

> *Come with me, my love*
> *To the sea, the sea of love*

It feels like a leaving and a returning; a descending and a lifting; a dropping and a rising into something that's maybe sleep or maybe death or maybe something else entirely – and it all feels good.

When I come to, Mrs Sullivan is smiling.

'Do you want to see?' she says. I look at her, and she smiles again. 'It's strong stuff, that gas. It can take a bit of time to wake up out of it. I'll give you a minute.'

I look at my arms: they are my arms. Or rather: they look like my arms. I put my hands to my mouth, my mouth that is so numb. I run my finger along the underside of the fangs. They feel sharp, but they don't feel as if they belong to me.

Mrs Sullivan reaches over and passes me a small hand-mirror.

'Have a look,' she says. 'What do you reckon?'

I can't quite move my lips yet, so I lift my top lip with my fingers, then look at my reflection. And there, what I've wanted for so, so long: two, white, sharp fangs.

'Unreal,' I say.

I ask to use the bathroom, and in the mirror above the sink I try to pull faces. But my mouth is still so numb, like the paused rictus of someone who has just suffered a stroke. It's astonishing that the procedure happened without my really knowing, without me really being there. She could have done anything to me while I was under. It's as if I've lost something, that when my days are finally tallied, part of today will be missing.

I urinate and there's something about the colour of my urine that seems off. It looks almost green. I flush, and when I flush, the toilet water keeps coming, keep gushing; I can hear the cistern filling and filling. This happens at home sometimes, so I know what to do. I remove the lid from the cistern, and inside the cistern the water is green and there is a laminated handwritten sign that says IN HERE GLYN. I reach my hand down into the water, until it's up to my elbow, and I can feel something, something metal at the bottom. I lean in and reach further, and then I pull out a key. Behind the toilet I see a small door now. I twist the key in the lock and the door opens, and I crawl into the small space, and I crawl on my hands and knees, and I am suddenly back in Caerphilly.

I always knew there was somewhere else, another realm behind all this. I heard it at night; I would stand on the road and hear the waters in the sewers underneath the concrete. There was something else going on, down there, I just knew it. I always imagined lifting the drain and there'd be a ladder. I would descend the ladder and there'd be darkness. There would be a moment then – a moment when I feel anything could happen – and it does:

A little light comes on, and I see them, waiting for me, my people.

I approach the group, and there is Alice. She looks more or less the same, though her hair is shorter. She is standing beneath a bare lightbulb. It's dark down here, but I can see walls, dark walls covered in grime and slime, and a series of old machines, servers I presume, with thick cables running between them.

'You've arrived,' Alice says, and the others in the group smile. They stand a little behind her, they are standing very still.

'How long have you been here?' I say.

'For as long as you've been an idiot,' she says.

'What?'

'We've been watching you since the start.'

'What do you mean?'

'You've suspected it for years, haven't you? That this life is unreal? That there is no way any of this could really be happening.'

'Where've you been all this time?' I say. 'Did you go back home?'

'It's like your laptop, Glyn. On the desktop, there are icons, right? – an icon for folders, files, applications. Well, those icons aren't the files themselves, are they? They're just visual representations, stand-ins for how things actually are.'

The group continues to smile, continues to stand still.

'And how things actually are, Glyn, well, none of this – your leather jacket, these fangs, your sense of self – none of these things are real, boy. None of us are real, either. The woman playing your mother has wanted out for a long time. You've made her so fucking depressed, Glyn. It's one of the worst cases we've ever seen.'

'Why doesn't she leave then?' I say.

'She can't, Glyn. That's not how it works. She has to stay there until you do something, until you make some change.'

'She drains *me*, though. You know that. It's why I'm so tired all the time. She saps me.'

'Have you ever thought that you drain *her*, Glyn? That it's the other way round?'

I haven't, but I know that would be the wrong answer.

'You should have done something by now, Glyn,' she says. 'You should have tested the system harder. But no, you just went into yourself, started wearing a leather jacket, started reading a whole load of shit about vampires, and thought that getting your teeth sharpened would change everything. How foolish do you have to be to think that getting fangs would solve all this?'

'I just wanted to feel part of something.'

'You feel weak, don't you?'

'You know I do.'

'And you think the fangs will give you strength?'

'It's a start, Alice. You have to give me that. Come on, at least I am trying to make a change.'

Alice walks away, but the group don't move. I follow Alice. She climbs up the ladder, and now I'm on the street, back in Caerphilly, and I can't see her any more, and I am passing the neighbouring venues of body modification – the tanning salon and the gym – and I am passing the vet's that used to be a video store, and inside the vet's I can see Mother, I can see her through the walls, she is standing in the surgery, standing over Margaret's body, I can see her and—

There goes Margaret, she is floating above the vet's; and there is Mother again now, at the living-room window, twitching the curtains, waiting for my return—

What does it mean to me, this person, this house?

A part of myself has been disconnected since childhood. There's a plug somewhere that needs to be put back in, to sync up all the different Glyns—

I want to be a part of things; I want to be together; I am not together—

Let me be a part of things—

Oh please, please, please let me feel—

I cry, I let out a moan, and find myself chanting, 'What am I? Who am I? Why?'

And then I'm in the dentist's street again, and I go through the side gate to the garden, and I walk into the shed, and I move past the wheelbarrow and the shovel, and I stride through, to the back of the shed, and I lift up the old brown rug, and I climb down the ladder, and I'm back in the bathroom.

'It's okay,' Mrs Sullivan is saying. 'It's okay, it's okay.'

She is kneeling beside me, on the floor, holding my hand.

'You've had a strange turn, a late reaction, that's all.'

She brings me up to her kitchen and makes me a cup of tea. She tells me stories about other vampires, about how the gas made one woman laugh hysterically for an hour afterwards. She had to put music on loud, so that the neighbours wouldn't get suspicious.

'How's the tea?' she says.

'Good,' I say.

'I'd make you some Marmite on toast, but you shouldn't eat for a few hours yet.'

She takes a sip of her tea then, and looks at me for what feels like a very long moment.

'What?' I finally say.

'I was just thinking,' she says. 'It's a funny life, isn't it? I was born a long time before you, in a completely different country, and now here we both are in this kitchen, drinking tea. Isn't that funny?'

I nod and go to say something about the nature of time, about how there is no 'now', because all this has already happened and will keep happening and—

'Anyway,' she says. 'I should take that money off you, before we forget.'

'Oh right,' I say. 'Of course.'

'It's £130.'

'You said £120 in the email.'

'Did I? Oh, fair enough: £120 then. Yes, £120 will do just fine.'

I take the envelope from my pocket, and she watches as I count the notes out onto the table.

'Lovely,' she says, though she doesn't touch the money. 'Thank you very much.'

When I go to leave, she offers me a lift home. I tell her no, but she is adamant.

'You had quite the shock,' she says. 'Please say yes. It would put my mind at rest.'

'Okay then,' I say.

'Good man,' she says.

When we pull out of her street, she puts on an old tape.

'Do you know Van Morrison?'

'I don't,' I say.

'Oh he's wonderful,' she says. 'He was one of my husband's favourites.'

We move through the streets, and in the mirror above the dash I keep checking my teeth.

'You're alright,' she says. 'They're still there.'

'They're just so real,' I say.

'I'm quite proud of them myself,' she says. 'But really, as soon as you can, you do need to come back for the sake of those molars. One of those teeth is literally rotten.'

We drive through Nantgarw, past the cinema, and I think of this morning, of how long ago it seems since the bus, and the driver, and even longer still since Mother and the cake, and the whole putting-me-into-a-memory-stick incident. There are some days that come and go like the blink of a cursor, while others play out for years, and keep playing, long after the day has passed.

When I ask Mrs Sullivan to drop me off on Nantgarw Road, she says she wants to bring me all the way home. She says she wants to make sure I get back safely.

'Please,' I say. 'I would really like to just walk for a little bit. It's only a five-minute walk.'

'Well, if I've learned one thing today,' she says – and she checks the wing mirror, then flips the indicator – 'it's that there's no point arguing with you.'

She pulls up outside Carpet Castle, up on the pavement, and as I take off my belt she turns to me: 'One thing before you go, though.'

'Yes?'

'I want you to smile at least once before you go to bed this evening. You are allowed to be happy, you know.'

'Okay,' I say, and I thank her, and I imagine reaching over and hugging her. In another spacetime, maybe I do hug her, but I won't here, not in this life.

'Have a good day,' I say.

'You too,' she says, and then I get out the car and begin the walk home.

As I stroll, I run my tongue along the bottom of my fangs and keep opening and closing my mouth. Have I changed? Have the teeth changed me? There's a vampire social in Whitby next month. I've wanted to attend for a few years now, but I've never felt ready. Since the whole Alice debacle, I haven't known how much of what I think or feel is real. After Alice, I realised that people will you tell you anything if it means they can get something in return. But now I know the truth; now I know that there is something beneath all this, beneath this surface world, and that there is something solid to the things I think and feel.

Passing under the bridge at Aber station, I think if thoughts are physical, if they are in some way material, then there is something solid to the shape of our ideas, and when we die and are buried, our final thoughts will be absorbed into the soil. But then again, if I am actually a vampire – if all that is real as well – then I'm already, in a sense, quite dead.

On Pontygwindy Road, when I'm almost home, one of the teenage boys who always shouts abuse at me is sitting on the wall outside Cheng Wong's. He's eating a carton of chips. He's actually surprisingly scrawny for someone with a diet so poor. He actually looks a bit like me before I started secondary school, before my screws were loosened and I lost my mind.

I go to cross, but there are cars coming both ways.

'Count Fucktard!' he shouts. 'Bum any kids today?' Behind him, the sun is brighter than it should be for October. The technicians have made a small error, perhaps. The sun feels warm, though; I feel it on my cheeks. It's been a long time since I felt the sun like this, since I've felt plugged in. Reaching into my inside pocket, I extract my sunglasses and put them on. Underneath this road, down in the sewers, they're gathering, my people are waiting for me.

The boy says: 'Are you a faggot paedo or do you screw little girl-goths, too?'

I approach the boy, and he looks uneasy, confused at my approach. I rest a hand on his shoulder, but he pushes it away. Slowly, very slowly, and pausing deliberately, with all the dramatic effect I can muster, I open my mouth – and smile.

'What the fuck!' he says. 'Have you got fangs?'

And with a swoosh of my leather jacket, I move between two cars, cross the road, and open my gate. It is lunchtime, and Margaret needs her walk.

Author note

I'd like express here my gratitude to the following artists:

Jane Deasy, for her composition 'Close to the surface'.

Sean Edwards, for his exhibition *Undo Things Done* (and accompanying art book), which I encountered at the Senedd in Summer 2021.

David Berman, for all of his poems and all of his songs.

Diolch yn fawr

For all their care on and off the page, diolch: Danny, Gill, Lisa Owens, Sally – seriously, thank you so much. Neither I nor the book would be here without you. For kindnesses too long to list, and for all the conversations, diolch: Will, Hilary, Winnie, Marta Kowalewska, Andrew Cowan, Lisa Mc, John & Aodh, Mick Magee, John Patrick, John Prasifka, Hannah Griffiths, Marcel, Sylvie and Enzo, Amy, Andy & Ada, Sunny Dragomir, Liz Fitzgerald, Gavin, Colin, Declan, Sean O'Reilly, Marie-Helene & Ted, Chetna, Jacinta, Rebecca Ivory, Zakia, Rahul & Polly, Sharon Love, Elena P, Judith & Alastair, Ruth McCourt, Joana Kelly, Liam & Maria, Nicole & Sean, Amy Heron, Tim, Sam, Cal, Gemima Salt, Lizzy Stewart, Rowenna, Emily Conlon, Kimberly Reyes, Sophie Hatch, Toby, Dave O'Dwyer, Rachel Bradbury, Luan and Sonny.

Diolch dearest Tracy for all your patience, guidance, and belief. Diolch Louisa for such wise stewardship these last five years; and thank you everyone at Faber for making this book a real thing. For supporting my writing: diolch Martin Doyle, John Lavin, Nina Herve & Will Burns, Becky Rip-ley. For letting me live in your beautiful homes: diolch Anne Legge, Gemma and Cai. For allowing me to work with you: diolch UCC, and Cliodhna and everyone at Temple Bar Gallery & Studios. For an evening I still think about: diolch i'r Adran Saesneg, Bangor. Am agor y drws: diolch o galon, Mr Huws a Mrs Mathias. For their hope-sustaining financial support: diolch An Chomhairle Ealaíon & Llenyddiaeth Cymru. For putting me back together again: diolch Olwen. Big love to: Dave, Roisin and DJ. I'r bechgyn YesCymru: Berwyn, Arwel, Lloydi – Ymlaen!

Ac wrth gwrs, diolch Mam, Laura, Lloyd, Louise, a Gwenann.

This book is for my mother, who told me I knew more.
I'm sorry that I almost drove you mad.